T0156415

One
Home Run

Art Voellinger

iUniverse, Inc.
Bloomington

One Home Run

iUniverse books may be ordered through booksellers or by contacting:

iUniverse
1663 Liberty Drive
Bloomington, IN 47403
www.iuniverse.com
1-800-Authors (1-800-288-4677)

ISBN: 978-1-4620-1066-0 (sc)
ISBN: 978-1-4620-1068-4 (dj)
ISBN: 978-1-4620-1067-7 (ebk)

Printed in the United States of America

iUniverse rev. date: 5/23/2011

Chapter I

The lyrics of "Night and Day" allowed the driver to hum, share the melody with a Chicago radio station, and reminisce as he turned his well traveled, 1948 black, Buick Roadmaster onto the college campus in northern Indiana.

Reducing the volume with his right hand and then pushing the peanut bag on the passenger side farther back in the seat, he wondered if this trip in early May to scout another ballplayer would be like many others. See a player, recommend him, or place his name on file had become a repetitious routine only a lover of baseball could endure.

Thanks to playing in one professional baseball season after returning from the War, "WW II" as he referred to it, he had met R. W. Johnston, a pitcher whose career lasted much longer than that of his roommate, the catcher who too often blocked home plate too well.

As the song reached "only you beneath the moon and under the sun," he wound through the campus while visualizing the play in a Class D game at Fort Wayne that changed his life.

On a summer night in the lowest level of baseball's minor leagues, he had awaited an outfielder's throw through a steamy haze hovering over the field in the late innings. After clutching the one-hop throw, he leaned to his left in an attempt to block the runner's slide and make a tag only to hear a pop louder than the umpire's call of "out!"

Unfortunately, the aggressive play also featured a torn cartilage resulting in a road map of stitches on the catcher's left knee - a type of autograph marking the end of a pro baseball career.

Yet, the catcher was lucky because of R. W. - Richard Waldo Johnston, who achieved what was called a "cup of coffee" with Cleveland in the major leagues, and later married the daughter of a team executive. Regardless if from friendship or pity, the catcher became a scout and had a job in baseball.

"Another Mickey Mantle" were neatly penned words of a letter partially visible from beneath the peanuts.

As the former catcher turned scout drove past a sign proclaiming "St. John's College" and into a parking space in front of a one-story building, he ignored the reference to the sensational New York Yankees outfielder in deference to a note paper clipped to the letter.

"Charlie, please take a look and phone me ASAP. Regards, R. W."

"What college kid could be like Mantle?" thought the scout.

For Charlie "Peanuts" Becker, being a left-handed batter with power was enough for a Cleveland scout to offer $500 and a bus ticket to the minor leagues. But that was in 1945, and the strapping youth from the Hoosier State never recalled being compared to a Yankee.

After taking a light-weight jacket from the back seat and a worn brief case and folding chair from the trunk of the Buick, Cleveland scout Charlie Becker realized he was being watched but did not hesitate to approach his observer.

"Baseball field around the corner?" he asked a coed whose wholesome appearance stood in contrast to the weathered, brick building which served as a recreation center at St. John's.

"Down that path and around the back of the building," she said as her sun glasses reflected Charlie's stare but not thoughts that had him comparing her to beauties seen only in magazines or on movie theater screens.

"Oh to be in college," he said to himself while admiring each step of the leggy blonde's ascent on stairs leading to the roof top. In addition to serving as a baseball vantage point, the flat surface provided a place to soak in sunlight on a Saturday that erased a winter of memories.

Chapter 2

The finely ground gravel path he took was a first for Charlie, who had no previous need to visit St. John's. Like many other small Indiana colleges, this was a place known more for basketball than baseball. And, as he viewed the playing field that distinguished itself only because its outfield fence looked like the red snow fences he'd seen along two-lane highways, he again understood why he had never been there.

Looking directly toward the north, he knew the wind originating off Lake Michigan less than a hundred miles away could make games more suitable for kite flying than baseball. However, on this day, the noon sunlight contributed to baseball on a field cut from a farm pasture a half century ago but displaying the required home plate, bases and pitching rubber.

"Baseball is baseball," thought Charlie as he approached small metal bleachers behind a backstop that was a far cry from the setting in Chicago where the Indians would be playing the White Sox in a major-league game.

After stationing himself in the first row of the bleachers, he placed his folding chair in a position so that it became a holder for his valise featuring the Indian head of the Cleveland logo. Reaching into a pocket of his jacket, he removed the St. John's schedule and roster R. W. had sent.

St. John's vs. Valparaiso had an interesting ring since it meant a Catholic college opposing the representatives of a Lutheran-based university.

"Would the Pope throw strikes past Martin Luther?" he wondered.

After introducing himself to coach Barton Griffin of St. John's as his team prepared for infield-outfield practice, Charlie sensed the rivalry and its level of intensity.

"Let's get these bastards," said a player with lowered head as he laced his spikes while seated on the long player bench on the third base side.

With rosters in hand, Charlie looked for the name of Randy Wilson as the St. John's starters took the field. Listed third in the batting order and playing center field was No. 27, Wilson, whose particulars had been scribbled on the back side of the roster by his coach in response to the scout and their first meeting.

"Junior, Bats: Left – Throws: Left, 5-11, 180 pounds, Crown Point, Indiana," was limited information preceding equally brief verbal info, including "good kid, .350 hitter, fast, with power, and a strong throwing arm."

The bespectacled, scholarly-looking coach did not have enough pre-game time to expand on Wilson, but Charlie did not mind.

A nine-inning game would allow for enough at-bats not only for him to observe players from both teams, but to appraise the outfielder whose initials were the same as another R. W., but whose talent had best be superior.

In the absence of batting practice, infield-outfield practice provided Charlie with an eye-witness assessment of Wilson's throwing arm. Time and again he threw on-the-fly to second and third base, and both of his throws to home plate sailed past the first baseman as a cutoff target and to the catcher on one bounce.

By then, the scout had adjusted his sun glasses and reached into his valise for a notebook on which he began a player profile. After the first and third innings, he noted how the left-handed batter turned on fast balls thrown by the tall Valparaiso pitcher for first a line drive single and then a double to right center field.

If the logo on his valise and his position behind home plate had not been enough for the handful of fans to determine that a scout was in attendance, Charlie provided final proof when he revealed a stop watch.

No need to double check on the 3.4 seconds the watch recorded. Wilson's home to first base speed was as evident as the enthusiasm he showed after a steal of second in the first inning. A base on balls in the fifth inning prevented additional timing but did reveal the batter's patience and ability to avoid swinging at pitches out of the strike zone.

In the eighth inning, a left-handed Valparaiso relief pitcher's curve ball seemed logical. But when it hung in space, Wilson snapped his wrists and forearms through the ball that landed well beyond a 330-foot sign attached to the fence in right field.

Subsequent screams from the sun-soaking coeds atop the recreation building were related not only to the 5-4 lead St. John's had taken but to the toss made by a student who had walked between the fence and the building, retrieved the home run ball, and preferred lobbing it to the roof rather than back to the playing field.

"Over 400 feet. Off a left hander," Charlie wrote as Wilson touched home plate and returned to his cheering teammates.

Chapter 3

Despite taking a one-run deficit into the ninth inning, the visiting team had to be pleased after a two-out base on balls and an infield throwing error placed runners at third and second base, representing the tying and potential winning run.

Expect a starting pitcher on the first 80-degree day of the spring to ignore the pressure of recording St. John's first victory over Valparaiso in 10 years, and the home team had earned its jitters.

One pitch, and one swing resulting in a long, line drive to left center field brought Charlie to the edge of his seat and closer to the screen where he was about to learn more about Randy on the ball field where the player's personal life could not be revealed.

More pre-game time would have allowed Charlie to speak with coach Griffin, who was told in September that his 20-year-old junior center fielder would be on his own regarding much of his future.

The only child of Tom and Claire Wilson of Crown Point, Randy had a typical childhood as a result of Tom working in the maintenance department of a Gary, Indiana, steel mill and Claire adding a wage as a cafeteria worker for CP High.

Had it not been for complications during her pregnancy, Claire would have had another son - two years after Randy's birth, but premature delivery was followed shortly thereafter by the infant's death.

The Wilsons never dwelled on the baby's death or Claire's hysterectomy, preferring to relish Randy, who learned work had rewards. Whether from odd jobs or summer employment, including at the steel mill, he accumulated enough money to purchase a 1949 Ford prior to his junior year at St. John's.

At the crack of the line drive off the bat of the burly, right-handed cleanup batter, Randy pivoted to his right and sprinted toward a spot past the 405-foot sign in deep center field.

Aware of the two-out situation and the score, the speedy runner at second base knew he would have little trouble scoring the lead run if the ball fell for a gap double or possibly a triple. And, like the third base coach, the runner envisioned the high blast winning the race.

Returning to college became a routine Randy enjoyed as a junior because his purchase of the used Ford allowed him to avoid having his parents drive him back to campus. Comfort came to a halt two weeks into the first semester when he received an early-morning knock on his dormitory door and was informed by a St. John's priest about a house fire the previous night in Crown Point. And, yes, his parents had perished in their totally destroyed, conservative wooden frame home.

For Randy, returning home meant first hand observations of the remnants of an apparent gas line leak and subsequent explosion whose flames also engulfed the one car garage and its contents. Within three days, he also faced the rigors of a wake and funeral. Other details would have to be handled by phone, mail, or by a visit at the semester break.

Resuming work toward a bachelor's degree in physical education allowed him to consider a future that could include coaching and teaching on the high school level rather than working in a steel mill.

Although St. John's had a coed enrollment of nearly 1,000, the 230 women considered part of the total student body either lived in the only women's dorm on campus or commuted from nearby communities. Once an all-male school, St. John's had followed the lead of some eastern colleges in opening its doors to women, but for Randy, a "hello" or "how you doing?" were about the extent of his words with women. Dating had not been a priority even in high school where playing basketball and baseball held his interest while he agreed with Dad's advice of "they can wait".

As a result of being left handed and wearing his glove on his right hand, Randy knew if he ran fast enough, he might have a chance at catching the ball - even if after a head-first dive.

He had made diving catches before on the sandlots of Crown Point, but never faced the challenge offered by the presence of an outfield fence.

First the dive. Then, the extended glove hand, and a catch that would be a game-winning grab if he could maintain his grip of the ball as he crashed not only into the fence but into one of the shoulder-high metal stakes that helped tie together the vertical sections of red wood.

Popular with his college classmates and easily recognized by his piercing blue eyes, blond flat top hair cut, and deep dimple in his left cheek, Randy enjoyed a college life that had him involved as an intramural captain of his dorm team in touch football and in basketball.

Academically, he felt secure after being told at the start of his junior year by a St. John's counselor, "You're on track to reach your goals" while referring to the P.E. degree and a national need for teachers and coaches. Playing baseball on a partial scholarship had helped reduce costs, but the sport was not as important as becoming the first person in his father's or mother's family to earn a college diploma.

Randy's catch of the line drive had a whiplash effect. After clawing the ball in the web of his glove, he became draped over the fence which buckled but fought to straighten itself because of the stakes that had served as security.

In the process of being knocked back to the outfield surface, the center fielder experienced more drama as a stake dug into the right side of his face. However, after falling backward, he was able to hold his glove high enough for an umpire to see its contents and signal the out.

Helped from the field by an assistant coach, Randy ignored blood dripping from the towel he had been given and relished the cheers of victory as he was led to the St. John's campus infirmary where he was lucky to have a doctor available.

Chapter 4

A two-story, white brick building, St. John's infirmary stood within a short walk of the middle of campus where prominent features were a reflecting pool with flowing fountain and a five-story administration building housing most of the undergraduate classes.

After walking across the front porch and into the lobby of the infirmary, Charlie had no trouble finding Randy because of the voices he heard coming from a room at the end of the hallway.

When Charlie peeked into the room, he saw Randy still in uniform and lying on his back. The scout was not surprised to find a doctor stitching the right cheekbone area of the player's face as a nurse responded to the visitor, "No concussion, nothing broken, just stitches."

As the doctor proceeded, Charlie found a seat in the hallway where he was joined by coach Griffin, who indicated the team had only one week and two games remaining, and there would be no need to return the center fielder to the playing field.

"We're 10 and 12, out of the conference race, and exams are right around the corner" said Griffin, who emphasized that his decision was not being influenced by Charlie's presence or a desire to see more of Randy in action. Meanwhile, since both men had time to discuss the player's past, including the deaths of his parents, the future became a topic.

According to Griffin, Randy could remain at St. John's during the summer, find campus employment, and live in the second story of the infirmary during the time when the dorms would be cleaned, disinfected, and prepared for another year.

Fortunately, Charlie had an alternative - one he thought of after watching the game. He would phone R. W. Johnston with more than a report. The center fielder's efforts were enough to cause Charlie to consider where Randy could play during the summer - something that appealed to the coach.

After being dismissed by the doctor, Randy continued to apply an ice bag to his face which revealed contrasting features, swelling on one side and a dimple on the other.

Taking a place on the porch with his coach and the scout, Randy learned of the proposal. Charlie would phone a friend in southern Illinois and seek a place for Randy to play as well as a place of employment.

With no home to return to, Randy welcomed a change of scenery and a chance to play in a men's league where improving his skills could lead to a summer visit by the scout. After providing his dorm phone number where he could be reached once Charlie had finalized arrangements, Randy shook hands with the scout and headed back to the baseball locker room where he discarded his dirty, blood-stained uniform.

By then, both the player and the scout could look ahead - Randy to a wholesome meal in the school cafeteria, and Charlie to the Buick where the remainder of a bag of peanuts would have to suffice until he reached his home in Indianapolis.

After a near two-hour drive south of St. John's, Charlie would have a cold cut sandwich and a beer and turn on his radio to learn the major-league scores. On the next day, Sunday, he would compile words and statistics for his report to Cleveland. His boss also would learn of the plans for the center fielder who within one game had become a prospect.

Chapter 5

From Collegeville, Indiana, the post office address of St. John's, Randy drove his Ford onto Route 24 and west into Illinois where he would follow Route 66 to southern Illinois.

He had heard the lyrics of the 1946 song "Get Your Kicks on Route 66," and hoped the directions provided by Charlie on a road map would take him to baseball kicks in areas known only by a well-traveled scout.

Finding his destination, Ashville, Illinois, might be easy, but once there, his challenge was to locate the Champion's Sporting Goods Store and its owner, Mr. Edward Champion, who had been contacted by Charlie and had multiple reasons to welcome Randy.

En route, Randy had reason to relax and enjoy the warm June air curling through the side windows of his car. Exams were over and before departing from St. John's, he had briefly returned to Crown Point to complete the necessary paper work related to his parents' deaths.

As estate executor and with the aid of a home town lawyer, Randy closed bank accounts and a safety deposit box containing his parents' will. He also paid funeral expenses, and learned he would receive a small settlement from insurance and the will. Add that money to his scholarship at St. John's, and he could look to a paid senior year when the expenses incurred by driving to Brook, Indiana, as a student teacher would be covered by whatever he had saved from his summer work.

He was on his own, a fact he had never envisioned although as a youngster he realized he had limited family. The only other Wilsons he knew of were an uncle (his dad's brother) in Michigan, and an aunt (his mom's sister) in Wisconsin, but both had died before Randy entered college.

After turning the Ford to the south off "24", he ran an index finger across the scar left by the removal of 16 stitches and paid more attention to the scenery along Route 66.

From Bloomington to Lincoln to Springfield, "66" stretched like a tightly pulled string through Illinois flat land graced by an early growth of corn.

Previously, he had experienced limited travel. As a youngster, he had vacationed with his parents to Michigan and Wisconsin and later traveled with his dad to sporting events in Chicago and Indianapolis, and even a football game at Notre Dame in South Bend. When he was in college, baseball trips provided a welcomed geographic change.

St. John's schedule included games against nearby opponents in Indiana and northern Illinois, but Randy especially enjoyed the bus rides as part of what SJC called its "spring trip" south to Evansville, Indiana; Cincinnati, Ohio, and Louisville, Kentucky.

As he drove, his comfort became linked to being able to reach Springfield and a city route which allowed for lunch and refueling. The Ford had become his prized possession. Thanks to one of his dad's friends being an auto dealer, Randy learned the car had been traded in by an owner whose retirement bonus sparked a desire for a more expensive car.

Considered revolutionary when it came off an assembly line as a flathead V8 with trademark front grille, this '49 Ford appealed to Randy not only as his first car, but because its red nearly matched the dominant red of St. John's school colors.

"Get Your Kicks" he thought while considering what fun existed in locations like Farmersville, Litchfield, or Mount Olive. Eventually, the sight of homes and buildings on the horizon and signs indicating "St. Louis" and then "Collinsville" meant he was approaching his destination.

Chapter 6

The road from Collinsville to Ashville was a direct route through areas that grew in population with each mile. Eventually, Randy reached a fountain - a War Memorial in the center of a circle of traffic although he later would learn the area was called the "Square".

Had Randy not followed the traffic flow, he would have circled the fountain more than once as he tried to determine which direction would lead him to Champion's. Fortunately, he made a three-quarter loop, and turned onto East Main Street where he noticed a movie marquee indicating "Stalag 17," starring William Holden. Finally, he arrived in front of a two-story building whose face featured a huge Champion's Sporting Goods sign over an entrance where the store windows displayed baseball equipment and the jerseys of high school, collegiate, and professional teams.

After parking on the opposite side of the street, he placed the directions from Charlie on the front seat, and walked toward the store where a glance at his reflection had him briefly thinking he was a mannequin amongst the jerseys. "Funny," he thought, "how a store window reflection allowed for musing in contrast to mirrors which provided the harsh reality of a person's face, including one that had been scarred."

At this point though, after a five-hour drive, he was satisfied with his appearance in Levi's jeans, a buttoned down white, short sleeve shirt, and penny loafers.

Hopefully, Mr. Champion would be inside, and Randy could learn additional details to go with the arrangements he had made with the scout.

"This either works, or I'm heading back to school," thought Randy, who had been assured by Charlie that their decision was sensible.

Near the front of the store, Randy introduced himself to a clerk, who appeared to be close to his age and height, but was thinner and wore a long sleeve shirt that looked more professional than comfortable on a day when the temperature hovered in the high 70s.

"He's upstairs," said the clerk while pointing with his right hand to a loft in the rear of the store where the owner and any other employees could look down on the customers and merchandise.

After walking through the first level that displayed rows of shotguns and rifles on one wall and sports equipment and uniforms on the other side, Randy followed steps to the second level. As he moved past the top step, he was greeted by a man whose strong handshake put a momentary hold on his visitor's apprehensiveness.

"Mr. Wilson, I assume," he said before leading Randy to a leather chair on one side of a desk featuring a gold plated "Edward Champion" name plate.

"Did you dance in Benld?" asked Champion while smiling in a way that returned Randy to apprehension since he had no knowledge of the community south of Springfield and just off Route 66. For years, the Benld Coliseum had hosted big bands in the largest (10,000 square feet) ballroom between Chicago and St. Louis.

Caught off guard by the Benld reference, Randy shifted in his chair and asked, "Is that what people do there?" before pausing and adding, "I've never been down here before."

"If all goes as planned, you'll learn about our area and more," said Champion while examining a letter signed by Charlie Becker.

"Charlie says you're going to be a senior in college, and should be able to help our team," said Champion.

"Had I known this sooner, I could have put you on our roster right away," he added.

More at ease after accepting the Coca-Cola bottle Champion placed in front of him, Randy explained how the scout had not seen him play until a couple of weeks ago.

"Since my parents are dead, he thought coming to Ashville would be an alternative to returning home where there is no summer baseball comparable to the men's league here," said Randy, who also was aware that Charlie had met Champion during previous scouting visits.

"All I want to do is play ball and work," said Randy, still anxious to learn about the arrangements.

"He thought it would be a good idea, and so do I," said Champion before adding that Becker's letter included more than statistics and indicated the scout would return to Ashville again this summer.

"You start work tomorrow morning," said Champion, whose experience as an owner and boss used to making decisions and giving directions led to a series which began with him pointing to a door to the right of his desk.

"That will lead you to your room on the left at the end of the hall. You can sleep back there and go in and out by the back door at the bottom of the stairs. There's a key to the door in the night stand. Rest room is across the hall. Park your car out back in our lot.

"My son Johnny is up front. He can help you bring in whatever luggage and clothes you have. No smoking, and no alcohol ever in here or your ass is back in Indiana!

"Report to Johnny in the morning, and he'll tell you what you're doing. Tomorrow's Tuesday. On Wednesday, we practice."

As Champion moved from his chair, Randy realized the owner who appeared to be in his mid-50s was over six foot tall and as physically imposing as his voice which grew in volume during a litany of instructions.

Standing, Randy reached for another hand shake which might have cemented their arrangement had it not been shortened by the ring of the telephone on the desk of the owner who pointed to the steps in a gesture of goodbye.

If Benld had been a vague reference, Champion's concluding words tied to work and baseball also lacked specifics. As Randy descended the stairs, he hoped Johnny could provide clarity.

Chapter 7

The only child of a demanding parent, Johnny Champion had become accustomed to remembering commands and retaining specifics.

As a result, within moments of returning to the front desk, Randy quickly learned Johnny's dad-given instructions indicating the collegian would work from 9 to 5 Monday through Friday with an hour off for lunch, would help in unloading supplies into the storage room at the rear of the store, would use the company truck to deliver product, would help at the front desk when necessary, and would be paid at a rate of $1.00 per hour.

"Two bits over minimum wage," said Johnny before repeating his dad's reference to practice on Wednesday and then giving directions to the home field of the team known as the Ashville Champs.

"You'll love right field."

Not wanting to delay seeing the field, Randy avoided telling Johnny he preferred playing center field and found his Ford for another drive around the War Memorial fountain. This time, he journeyed south five blocks to an intersection where a sign atop a wooden fence read "Ashville Athletic Field". Painted lower were words expressing "Home of the Champs".

After parking on a lot behind the ball park, Randy walked onto the concrete floor of the main entrance directly behind home plate. He quickly understood Johnny's reference to right field as he read four green outfield signs with white lettering indicating distances from home plate.

In left field, 330; left center, 355, and in dead center, 425. However, in right, a 305 sign hung near the top of a chain link fence standing about 20 feet high. The fence stretched another 40 feet from the right field foul pole to a scoreboard sitting atop part of the wooden fence which surrounded the remainder of the field.

In contrast to the wooden fence featuring advertisements, including Champion's Sporting Goods, the metal section permitted visibility of a creek that was responsible for the shortest outfield dimension because its banks curled just beyond the right field playing area.

Other aspects of the field included rows of wooden seats beneath a grandstand roof, concrete dugouts, and what remained of two light standards situated just beyond the fence in left center and right center. As Randy observed, he was startled by the deep voice of a man who exclaimed, "The flood did that."

Turning, Randy found himself just a few feet in front of a husky, dark haired man whose appearance might have shocked anyone because of his stubble beard, gapped front teeth, and considerably stained, short sleeve T-shirt, pants, and weathered brown shoes.

"The water knocked out the other poles," explained the man. "That's all that's left as proof we once had night baseball here."

"Had to clean the damn grill and get rid of the damn grease," he said while ignoring that Randy had no idea he had been approached by the owner of the Foul Ball Tavern located across the street from the left field side of the Athletic Field.

"Dutch Schmidt," said the man as he wiped his hands on his shirt and then extended his tattooed right arm toward Randy.

"Saw you pull into the parking lot," he said. "Come over to my place."

Once inside the Foul Ball, Randy knew he was in a baseball haven because framed autographed photos of major leaguers dotted the walls which surrounded tables and chairs in one area and a pool table in another.

Two hamburgers aided by a clean grill, an order of French fries, and a bottle of Coca-Cola satisfied Randy's hunger, but because of Schmidt's steady jabber, the Ashville newcomer learned more than he had expected.

According to Schmidt, the Athletic Field was called "Stag Park" for a few years after World War II when the Ashville Stags, nicknamed for a local brewery, were a Class D affiliate of the St. Louis Browns, who enjoyed having a minor-league team within an hour's driving distance of the major-league team's home offices.

"After the flood in 1950 knocked down part of the right field fence and the other light poles, the Browns never had enough money to help replace anything and moved their team out of here," said Schmidt.

"Word is they're going to move the big club to Baltimore."

"Had a hell of a business before the creek flooded, especially when the Browns played the Stags, or when the Stags played the Kansas City Monarchs or House of David in exhibition games," added Schmidt, whose speech was slightly affected by his use of chewing tobacco.

"Looks like everybody's going to have to follow the Cardinals now," he added, referring to the National League Cardinals, who shared Sportsman's Park in St. Louis with the American League Browns.

"Browns in Philadelphia tonight; Bob Turley's going to start," said Schmidt of the right hander who he said grew up in East St. Louis, had pitched for the Stags, and now was a big league rookie.

As Schmidt reached for a radio on the back bar, Randy realized the tavern owner had shown no curiosity regarding the visitor's age or background and was still rattling about baseball as a customer wearing a Cardinals' T-shirt and Browns' hat entered.

After telling Schmidt "thanks," Randy departed, returned to his car and began making plans for his first night in the room at Champion's while also looking to his first practice with the Champs

Chapter 8

After experiencing a good night's sleep and finding that the restroom across the hall from his bedroom included a shower and vanity, Randy also became more at ease as he followed Johnny's lead at work.

Additional confidence came after he donned practice baseball pants, a sweatshirt, and hat he had brought from St. John's and drove to the Athletic Field where he noticed other cars already parked.

It had been nearly three weeks since he had swung a bat, but the sunlight had him anticipating a two-hour practice as he grabbed two bats and a bag containing his glove and spikes from his car's trunk.

Once through the ball park's entrance, he found Edward Champion, who introduced Randy to Red Morrison. A tall, lean man in his early 60s, Morrison sported a red, well-worn baseball hat boasting "Champs".

"Best baseball man in the area," bragged Champion.

Retired after coaching at Ashville High School, Morrison claimed he had worn a ball uniform from the time he was nine years old.

"Put your stuff on top of the dugout, and I'll introduce you to the other guys when I get over there," said Morrison, who turned and spoke with Champion while ignoring that as Randy walked away, the newcomer could hear the conversation of the manager and the sponsor.

"Damn right we need him," said Morrison. "We've got too many guys in Korea."

"You've still got to take a look, but he's highly recommended," replied Champion without adding more about the Korean War which had led to three starting Champs' players being drafted.

As Randy approached the first base dugout, he drew glances from a group of a dozen men ranging in age from their 20s to 30s. Morrison's arrival for what Randy learned would be the team's last practice before playing Sunday was followed by names and handshakes and the manager urging the players to play catch prior to taking batting practice.

"Range, start warming up," barked Morrison before telling Randy, "You might be hitting third on Sunday if Champion can get you on the roster".

Apparently, the players had been previously informed of Randy's arrival since there were no looks of dissatisfaction related to Morrison's announcement.

Although the Champs had practiced twice weekly in late April and early May, they were beaten the previous weekend in a Memorial Day doubleheader at Millstadt where poor hitting contributed to non-league losses of 7-1 and 5-0.

However, from the first pop of the ball off Randy's bat, optimism spread, causing Edward Champion, seated in the area which once had served as box seats for the Stags, to lean back, take a long drag from a cigar, and blow a smoke ring.

Urged by Morrison to throw harder, Range complied. Randy responded by ripping pitches into the right field fence before lofting two balls high and long over the fence and into the middle of the creek.

"That's enough," said Morrison before directing Randy to center field where he could get accustomed to the Athletic Field while catching fly balls.

Later, Randy learned right hander Range's first name was Bob, and that he had pitched at Southeast Missouri State University before dropping out of school after his sophomore year to get married and work at the Ashville shoe factory.

After watching other players hit an occasional long fly ball off Range, Randy thought about the Champs' talent and wondered even more when he looked toward the dugout where Morrison was met by a late arriver.

"Last batter," yelled Morrison, who, while aware of a sudden wind and approaching clouds, told Range to throw from several feet in front of the pitcher's mound and to the backstop after his catcher had taken a place in the batting practice rotation.

Dressed in gray sweatpants and shirt and a hat similar to Morrison's, the broad shouldered, muscular, right-handed batter tossed a cigarette away, took two practice swings and strolled into the batter's box. What followed were line drives and long fly balls, including two off the left field fence.

"Could hit out of a snow bank," bellowed Morrison after another blast banged into the outfield wall moments before a flash of lightning and thunder and then rain forced the manager to shout, "Let's get the hell out of here! Everybody to the Foul Ball."

Chapter 9

Rain was not the only reason the Champs scurried to the Foul Ball. After placing his equipment in the trunk of his car, Randy sprinted across the street and entered the tavern where he found Johnny Champion seated at a table holding boxes containing white uniform pants, red-on-white, pin-striped shirts, red stirrups, hats, and belts.

"Over here," Johnny told Randy, who was about to learn more about the Champs and the St. Clair County League because the room included more than the players whose names were about to be called from a clipboard list.

After receiving a soda and a pat on the back from Dutch Schmidt, Randy noticed Edward Champion and Red Morrison seated with seven other men, including one who told the others, "Tonight's the first roster deadline, and we're not changing the damn schedule."

"League meeting," Johnny explained before calling the name "Frank Slade."

Imposing as the last batting practice batter, Slade, even at age 32, was equally impressive at the Foul Ball where he showed thick wrists and powerful forearms as he reached for a uniform and schedule from Johnny.

"See you Sunday," said Johnny before telling Randy that Slade was leaving to work a nightshift at the Ashville brewery.

As Johnny recorded each player's uniform number, Randy's attention was drawn elsewhere - first to the league table where baseball tales dominated the conversations, and then to the bar where Schmidt addressed a customer.

"Son of a bitch is tough," said Schmidt.

"They were shooting pool one Sunday after a game, and when that ass hole Brown kept riding him about not being good enough to play pro ball, he grabbed him with his left hand, took a pool stick with his right hand, and stuck it right beneath his jaw.

"Told him he'd either push it to his brain, or drop it, and kick his ass.

"Truth is he didn't have to do that because he could've hit him like Rocky Marciano and been done with it."

Even before Johnny interjected, "He's talking about Slade," Randy assumed the identity. However, he was not as quick to determine the topic raised by the largest of the men seated near Edward Champion.

"What in the hell is he doing on the roster?" asked the fat man who Johnny identified as Lee Mathews, president of the St. Clair League.

"I'll put whoever I want on the roster," said Champion. "He's my kid, goes to all the games, and I'll be damned if we'll ever forfeit anything because we don't have enough players."

"How the hell can he swing a bat?" asked Mathews, causing Randy to again observe Johnny's left arm and the handicap which accounted for the store owner's son wearing long sleeve shirts in order to conceal the arm.

Hesitant to ask about the arm, Randy need not question again thanks to Johnny.

"Fall out of a tree when you're a kid, have a limb break loose and follow you to the ground where it crushes your arm, and you're not worth a shit," said Johnny loud enough for the men at the other table to hear.

If Mathews had hit a foul ball at the Foul Ball, it mattered little to him because after being hushed by Johnny's comments, the president resumed directing the meeting. Meanwhile, Schmidt broke his silence by pouring another beer and starting another story for the visitor who Johnny identified as Walter Irish, sports editor of the Ashville News.

"He's here for a story," said Johnny of Irish, whose pencil mustache compensated for a receding hairline.

In his late 50s, Irish had been with the News since graduating from high school. After working his way up from copy boy to reporter, to sportswriter, he was one of the longest tenured members of the newspaper staff and easily identifiable by name or appearance.

Seldom seen in a suit or sports jacket, he wore white short sleeved shirts in the summer and often found as many mustard or ketchup stains as story tips at the Foul Ball. Blessed with keen powers of observation and an inquisitive mind that drove him to dig for information, he also had a passion for food and drink that contributed to his pot belly.

For Randy though, there was more concern about getting uniform No. 27 and receiving a schedule highlighting opposing teams and playing dates, including July 4 weekend games, July 26 all-star game, and August 30-September 6 playoffs. Rain, as noted, could affect all dates.

Chapter 10

If Randy thought he was the only person to understand why he had chosen uniform No. 27, he was wrong. Evidence came in the form of the Monday, June 22, edition of the Ashville News featuring a sports page headline: "Dandy Randy Leads Champs," a four-column photo of Randy crossing home plate after a game-winning home run against defending champion Freeburg, and an "Irish Brew" column headlined: "Hoosier Happy to be Here."

"I didn't expect this," said Randy as he handed the paper to Johnny at the Champion's front desk where a male customer added more of the unexpected by saying, "Happy Birthday. Hope you like it here. I look forward to seeing you play."

As the sports editor of the newspaper with the largest circulation in the southwestern Illinois Area discounting the East St. Louis Journal and two St. Louis dailies which covered the St. Clair League with scores only, Irish freely fed readers in Ashville's 20,000 population and throughout the outlying area. And, since the News did not publish on Sundays, he had extra time to find local stories.

The "Brew," no doubt, had inflated the customer's enthusiasm. In addition to detailing Randy's background and how he was led to the Champs, the writer referred to "the blond haired, blue-eyed center fielder whose 21st birthday on June 27 accounted for the selection of uniform No. 27".

After recognizing the Champs' 4-0 league start under "the crafty decision making of Red Morrison," Irish referred to the hitting of Wilson and third baseman Slade in the number 3 and 4 spots in the lineup, solid pitching by Range, and the defense of the brothers Anderson - Sandy at shortstop and Mark at second base.

"Add the versatility of outfielders Tom Bauer and Ray Smith, who also can serve as pitchers, to the steady play and occasional hitting of the other starters - catcher Vernon Koester and first baseman Ted Hill, and it appears the Champs can return to the glory of their last title in 1951," wrote Irish.

According to Johnny, Irish's interview of Randy after the dramatic home run far over the right center field fence was only part of the reason for the story and column.

"You've already hit four home runs, two doubles and a triple, and you're hitting .412," said Johnny.

"I didn't know he'd write my life history," responded Randy before adding, "at least he mentioned everybody's name."

In addition to becoming comfortable with his teammates' names, Randy learned the names of more communities offering competition for the Champs. Besides Freeburg, he became aware of New Athens, Lebanon, O'Fallon, Mascoutah, St. Libory, and Shiloh, but admitted he did not understand what SIP meant and never considered trying to find it on a map.

"Schedule shows us playing at SIP on Saturday," Randy said to Johnny, "Where's that?"

"Heck of a place to celebrate your birthday," said Johnny with a smile.

"It's not a city. It's the name of the Southern Illinois Penitentiary in Chester, and we play there every summer."

At practice on Wednesday, Randy learned that Edward Champion received $25 for bringing his team to the penitentiary.

"Just pack your uniform and be ready to go in the morning," said Johnny. "We leave at 8 o'clock from the front of the store."

Chapter II

Knowing baseball would be part of his day made Randy an early riser on the morning of his 21st birthday.

After bounding down the back stairs of Champion's and walking to the front of the store, he was not surprised to find his 8 a.m. arrival coinciding with that of a dark blue, 1953 Lincoln Capri. More surprising was seeing Johnny as the driver. Besides being able to reach the steering wheel with both hands, he was able to shift gears because of the car's automatic transmission. Also interesting was that Irish, who an hour earlier had closed the sports pages of another Saturday edition, sat in the back with Edward Champion.

Because of the Capri's design, the trunk was large enough to carry bags of bats and balls, catching equipment, and two gym bags - one displaying the name and colors of St. John's College and the other featuring a Champion's Sporting Goods Store decal on its side.

"We should be able to make it to Chester by 9," Champion told Johnny, who was reminded that the team would meet at the parking lot across from the entrance to the prison.

As Johnny drove the car toward the Ashville fountain, Irish was quick to ask Randy, "You ever been in a prison?"

The reply of "No" became reason for the sports editor's comments allowing Edward Champion to doze while Randy learned endless facts related to the Southern Illinois Penitentiary being built on 12 acres and opened in 1878 just outside of Chester in Randolph County.

"They've got about 2,000 inmates and a death row," said Irish. "Get the death sentence, and they can give you the electric chair."

"What about the baseball team?" Randy asked.

"That's part of their entertainment," said Irish, who explained how the prison team's players were the envy of the all-male population, including many who, if on good behavior, attended the games.

"No away games for this team," said Irish with a laugh which woke Edward Champion and caused the team sponsor to murmur, "Place has a lot of nuts."

"Maybe that's where Keller should have gone," said Irish with a change of subject that perked Randy's curiosity.

"Just as long as you didn't write about what he did," said Champion. "Slade didn't need any of your bullshit."

Hesitant to ask how Slade was tied to someone of questionable sanity, Randy need only listen.

"You know damn good and well Keller was obsessed with his son," Irish said to Champion.

"Everybody in town, including old man Keller, had heard you were looking for a third baseman if Frank's work would keep him from making it to all your games. So Keller brings the boy - Kent is his name - to a practice, you let Red work him out, and then you cut him."

As if caught by Irish's explanation of the events, Champion lowered the window to his left, breathed in the fresh air and responded, "His kid was no better player than Johnny would be," said Champion.

"Keller knew that all along, but Kent was his only son, and the old man kept trying to get him on a team - any team, even though he wasn't even good enough to make the high school team this year.

"Maybe that was it. Keller had to work when he was in high school and never played on any team, but his son was not going to go without getting to play baseball somewhere.

"The old man actually thought Kent was as good as George Kell of the Detroit Tigers, and even called him 'Kell' all the time instead of Kent because in his eyes, his son was an all-star like Kell. That boy must have had a million ground balls hit to him on the playgrounds near their house long before he came to our practice.

"Funny thing was the kid could field a ground ball, but he couldn't throw worth a damn, and when we gave him a chance to hit, he took a dozen swings before hitting anything out of the infield.

"I told Keller to let the kid alone, but he couldn't do it, and one night his mind must have flipped because he went into his garage, put a hose from the exhaust pipe of his car through the window on the passenger side, and then turned the ignition key.

"By the time his wife came out of the house looking for him, he was slumped over the steering wheel.

"Cops told me the car radio was on when they got there, and the announcer was giving accounts of the Browns game against Detroit."

For the first time during the drive to Chester, Irish kept silent. However, the hush was short lived as Johnny turned the Lincoln into the parking lot across from the prison and exclaimed, "Hey, there's Dutch!"

As the tavern owner waved, Edward Champion glanced at a letter from the prison athletic director reminding the Champs to bring players, a scorekeeper, and only what had been termed "responsible adults" into the prison.

"Let's see what's inside," said the elder Champion as a guard met the group outside the main gate and told them to form a single file.

Chapter 12

Although the gate to the prison's main entrance was part of a 10-foot high fence topped by barbed wire, the Administration Building through which the Champs had to pass offered an exterior whose architecture was similar to other stone structures posing as banks or governmental buildings in southern Illinois.

Had Irish taken more time to indulge Randy during their Route 3 journey which often provided views of the Mississippi River, the sports wag could have told of the 1952 riots at the prison. One, on October 27, escalated when more than 300 inmates in the East Cell House seized control, took seven guards as hostages, and made demands.

To quell the rebellion, then Illinois Governor Adlai Stevenson, the Democratic candidate for President in 1952, flew back from a campaign stop in Pittsburgh. After attempts to obtain the release of the hostages failed, about 100 prison guards and state police stormed the cell house, and the hostages were released unharmed.

Because this visit by the Champs was less than a year after the October riots, guards stationed outside and inside the Administration Building provided a sense of security which increased as other guards patted down each member of the group and searched through bags and belongings. Additional comfort came in seeing Edward Champion greeted by two men at the front of the line that took the visitors into a meeting room where the team sponsor introduced Warden Ross Randolph and Athletic Director Roger Wolff.

"We welcome you and remind you this is a state prison," said Randolph, whose gravelly voice carried a tone of command. "You are here to play ball, eat after the game, and remember the only way you want to come back here is as a baseball player."

As Randolph departed, Wolff asked the Champs to place their valuables in a metal box which would be locked in a vault. The AD then reminded all within listening distance, "Your team is one of the first we've had back in here since the riots, and we expect your behavior to be the best."

As visitors to the "pen," as Edward Champion called the penitentiary, the Champs had scored easy victories in 1951 and '52 and appreciated the cash stipend given to visiting teams.

"Regardless of what you see or hear out there, we're here to play baseball, and don't think just because they're convicts some of them cannot play," said Champion, who reminded the group that Wolff had been a major-league pitcher for seven years.

"1941 through '47," blurted Irish. "In '45, he won 20 games for the Washington Senators and was part of one of the strangest pitching staffs in baseball history because four of them threw knuckle balls."

Almost as if on cue due to previous trivial conversations, Edward Champion recited the names of Wolff, Mickey Haefner, Dutch Leonard, and Johnny Niggeling.

"Niggeling was from Iowa, but the others from Illinois," said Irish before tying Wolff to Evansville, Haefner to New Athens, and Leonard to Auburn, Illinois.

As the Champs walked down a hall and past a huge holding cell, they encountered a guard and entered a locker room. After putting on uniforms, they heard Red Morrison say that the batting order would be as usual but Bauer would do the pitching, and Range would play the outfield.

"Don't forget, we've got a league game tomorrow," said Morrison before handing a scorebook to Irish, a bat bag to Schmidt, and a ball bag to Johnny Champion, who stayed close behind his father as the Champs were led to the baseball field.

Chapter 13

Baseball diamonds can share similar characteristics, but when it comes to ballparks, there can be drastic differences since not all surfaces or grandstands are the same, and generally it's the outfield fence or lack thereof that distinguishes one field from another.

At the Southern Illinois Penitentiary, as the Champs click-clacked in their spikes past vacant wooden bleachers on the third base side, they became aware they would be playing within the largest wall of any ballpark.

"That thing's got to be a 100 feet high," said Johnny Champion while pointing to the wall that originally had been cut out of a limestone bluff when the prison was built.

Although the distance from home plate to the right field corner was not much farther than Ashville's Athletic Field, the wall extended not only into deep center field but around the entire prison. As the sharp points of barbed wire glistened from either side of a walkway, rifle-carrying guards moved from tower to tower while observing the baseball action or whatever went on in the area normally referred to as "the yard."

"Look in left field," Randy urged Johnny, whose jaw dropped not because of the metal fence and barbed wire serving as an interior left field wall, but because of the four, doorless outdoor commodes sitting in full view in foul territory.

"Holy shit!" said Johnny, drawing an "I doubt if that happens here" comment from Irish.

As the Champs warmed up by playing catch in front of the right field wall, Edward Champion, Morrison, Irish, and Schmidt engaged in conversation with Wolff near a row of benches on the first base side and in front of a fence separating the players from the bleachers.

"I'll be behind home plate," said Wolff before the "Bang! Bang!" of a bass drum and appearance of a handful of men wearing blue denim trousers and shirts and carrying musical instruments.

"That's our band," said Wolff. "We will have a National Anthem."

Shortly thereafter, a dozen men in gray baseball uniforms displaying "Cubs" printed in dark blue on their chest walked in single file to the third base bench. Once there, they were given gloves and balls to warm up with while the Champs took infield practice.

After the prisoners took their turn on the infield, it became apparent playing a game only once a week had affected their skills. In addition to wild throws from outfielders who seldom had a cutoff man to throw to, infielders not only had trouble fielding ground balls but were equally inefficient throwing to first base.

During the Cubs' ineptness, the wooden grandstands became a flurry of activity as convicts took their seats. Baseball was about to provide a distinct change from the drudgery of daily lives in a place where good behavior permitted watching a game on a sun-drenched Saturday.

"Everybody up," barked one of the two men dressed in white T-shirts and blue slacks who obviously were prisoners serving as umpires. In a much lower tone, Morrison urged the Champs to line up for a playing of the National Anthem, which featured enough off notes and squeaks of instruments by the time of the music's conclusion to arouse an ovation by spectators and players alike.

"Ever seen anything like this?" Johnny asked Randy.

"Never, and I never want to be in a prison again as anything but a visitor," said Randy, who might not have been so eager to play had he known what was ahead.

Chapter 14

Even before the first pitch, Randy and the Champs knew this would be a different kind of game.

For Johnny, it became an opportunity to not only wear a uniform but coach first base. His normal duties included being the bat boy but now were changed by the presence of a prisoner whose baseball cap contrasted with the short-billed, navy blue hats worn by the other convicts.

"Just call me Moon," he said as he knelt near the Champs' on-deck circle which had been as heavily chalked as the foul lines of the dirt infield and outfield.

"Moon Mason, best damn bat boy south of Chicago," he added before responding to a spectator's request to explain his style of wearing a baseball hat.

"Hat's bill follows the sunlight," explained Moon, whose mischievous eyes belied the joking personality he had developed during 20 years of prison life.

On the field, the Cubs (named after the Chicago Cubs) offered additional uniqueness in the form of a huge Negro pitcher whose 6-foot-5, 225-pound stature and rapid fast ball made the 60-feet, 6-inch distance from mound to plate seem much closer.

Entered in Irish's scorebook as "Heat Johnson," with an additional note of "he's new," the big right-handed pitcher became a focus of attention since he had never faced the Champs in previous summers.

Amazingly, all of his warm up pitches, including some in the dirt, were caught by a catcher wearing a face mask and chest protector, but only one shin guard.

"Kneels with the other knee," said Moon. "Why wear two shin guards when you only need one?"

Strikeouts of the Anderson brothers on blazing pitches drew roars from only a portion of the crowd of 500 - a fact causing Schmidt and Edward Champion to remind the Champs about the prisoners betting cigarettes on the action.

While waiting to bat, Randy was put at ease by Moon saying, "Don't worry, Heat's arm will wear down quickly."

But once in the batter's box, Randy wondered why Moon had not explained the smile that preceded a leg kick and a pitch which took a path directly at the batter's head.

Had it not been for Randy's quick reflexes, the ball would have struck his right temple. However, when he leaned back to avoid being hit, the ball still tore into his left elbow that had become exposed to the pitch.

"Take your base," said the plate umpire in a tone considerably lower than Wolff's, "Do it again, Heat, and I'll have you put in the hole."

After experiencing instant pain in his elbow and arm, and falling to the ground, Randy avoided looking at the pitcher and moved to first base where he encountered another well built Negro.

Urged by his college coach to avoid speaking with the opposition because they were the bitter enemy, Randy kept quiet. But the first baseman, whose scarred face was the result of a switch blade fight in Chicago, addressed Randy and asked, "Surely, you must know we read newspapers in here?"

"What the hell did you expect?" "Heat's a lifer. In here for murder."

If those words brought an unaccustomed tenseness to Randy, relief came in the form of Slade's hitting in the cleanup spot.

On Heat's first pitch, the Champs' power hitter launched a rocket that curved foul well in front of the left field fence but banged against the walls of one of the four commodes before rattling over and out above a toilet seat. Fortunately, that stall was vacant, but the adjacent commode's resident sitter drew the attention of spectators and players alike.

"Hey Nixon, did you drop what you were doing?" screamed one fan.

"Nixon almost witnessed a hole in one," said another.

As the laughter died, Heat threw another fast ball, and again Slade swung into the pitch. But this liner had less curve and was head high at Nixon. Unable to move from his commode because of his lowered pants, he ducked as the ball ricocheted off the back wall, past his head, and out onto the field.

As Slade stepped back out of the batter's box, he glared back at Heat. Meanwhile, Nixon responded to his hot seat by unrolling several sheets of toilet paper and waving them in the fashion of a white flag surrender.

Again, laughter prevailed until Slade cracked a shot in fair territory off the left field fence. His triple scored Randy and sparked a 10-1 rout aided by Bauer's ability to throw curve ball strikes.

Walked four consecutive times after being hit, Randy benefited from Wolff's threat but still had a swollen left elbow. Due to Slade's slugging after the base on balls, prisoner errors, and two hits each by the Anderson brothers, the Champs could relax at a post-game chicken dinner in the guards' mess hall.

"Make sure you get all your gear out of the locker room before we leave," said Edward Champion.

"We've got some stops to make on the way home," he added before Irish intoned, "and we've got a birthday boy with us."

Chapter 15

Small towns in southern Illinois are not spaced together like birds on a wire. The closeness comes in the fact that for every 20 or so miles there's a tavern whose location contributes to a familiarity unrelated to geography.

For a successful baseball team traveling on Route 3 and then onto Route 159 back to Ashville late on a Saturday afternoon, recognizing a 21st birthday became reason for celebration and camaraderie after defeating a prison team.

Fortunately for Randy, the first pit stop of the four-car caravan came as Irish concluded a story about a previous prison visit.

"If you think their catcher today was a bubble off, you should have seen their center fielder when Schmidt played before the war," Irish recalled.

"It had rained the night before, but they still wanted to play, especially since most of the water damage was in the center field area.

"So this guy plays without spikes because wearing them doesn't do him any good in the mud, and he isn't about to keep putting on his shoes and then taking them off.

"Sure enough, he gets a base hit, advances to second base, and then tries to score on a single only to have Schmidt, who was catching for us, step on one of the con's bare feet and spike him.

"The con not only was called out, but his right foot was bleeding, and he had to be carried off the field. Half of the prisoners cheered because they were betting on the prison team being shut out."

Irish had just uttered "shut out" when Edward Champion instructed Johnny to turn left toward the tavern whose side parking lot and front door were within view from the highway.

Once inside the Hunter's Corner, Edward Champion shook hands with the owner and informed the players that drinks were on the team sponsor. Seated at a table with Johnny, Randy stared in awe at the many deer heads and photos of smiling hunters adorning the walls. But he had little time to observe more after Irish placed a full mug of beer in front of him.

"Go ahead. You're 21, and it might ease the pain in your arm," said Irish as the players surrounded Randy with a chorus of "Happy Birthday".

Normally a soda drinker and seldom a drinker of alcohol which had been prohibited on St. John's campus, Randy had little choice after Irish made a toast saluting him. After a clicking of mugs for the "Hitting Hoosier" as he had been described in one of Irish's game stories, Randy experienced his first taste of Stag beer.

At the bar with Schmidt and the owner of the tavern, Edward Champion raised a glass and shook his head from side to side as a reminder to Johnny to remain alcohol free.

"Like Mathews said, 'If you can't drink beer and dance, you can't play in this league,' " said Irish in reference to comments made previously by the St. Clair president regarding the league's winter banquet and dance.

Satisfied by the all-you-can-eat dinner at the prison, the Champs fed their thirst rather than hunger. As they proceeded from the Hunter's Corner, additional stops allowed for everything from shooting pool, to playing pin ball machines, to watching card tricks by Schmidt.

Even if the beer seemed to reduce the pain in his left arm and elbow, Randy refrained from participating with his teammates. As a result, at the Do Drop Inn near Ellis Grove, he decided to speak with Slade, who supported his reputation of being a "loner" by sitting alone.

With his confidence boosted by working at the sporting goods store and meeting clients and customers, and by respecting his teammates' hitting exploits at the prison, Randy pulled a chair out from across Slade. The dark haired slugger seated behind a beer and a shot glass of whiskey frowned but did not object to Randy's presence or a question related to the prison pitcher's intentional wildness.

"Don't you ever get scared?" Randy asked.

Chapter 16

If Randy had expected baseball to dominate an answer to his question, he was wrong. And, if he had thought Slade unwilling to share thoughts, he was equally wrong.

"Was your dad in the military?" asked Slade. "Yes," said Randy as a waitress placed a fresh beer in front of him and added a bowl of pretzels which found Slade's grasp.

After taking a bite, Slade weighed the question, hesitated, put his head in his hands and continued speaking.

"I've been told about your parents, so I guess you already know about being scared."

"Did your dad talk about the War?" asked Slade.

"Only about some of the cities he saw," said Randy.

"Some guys never say anything, but you don't look like another Irish," said Slade. "No need for you to repeat what I tell you, but maybe you can learn something from it.

"I was 21-years-old and already in the Army for two years when we were in the Ruhr Valley and fighting the Germans in World War II.

"It was nearly dark one night, and I was in a fox hole about 100 yards or so from a farm house when Pea-Pot jumped in by me. Everybody knew Pea-Pot from when he was on KP duty. I can't remember his real first name. His last name was Jackson, and he was a dandy.

"The story I got was that he wasn't the smartest of guys, but he went from basic training to KP duty and then to delivering our mail. When he jumped in by me that night, I told him to keep his head down because the Germans could see us from that building and were within shooting range.

"I asked him, 'What the hell you doing here?' and he told me how he had bugged the chaplain, who bugged the captain, who bugged the platoon leader to finally let him be one of the troops.

"Sure enough, a few minutes later, he must have peeked from his position only to be shot right about here," said Slade while pointing to the center of his forehead.

"One of the last things I remember him saying was, 'Hey, I'm carrying a rifle now.' "

After taking a sip from his shot glass and then a larger drink of beer, Slade leaned back in his chair for a few moments, and, after coming forward, looked directly into Randy's eyes and resumed speaking.

"Pea-Pot's head was a mess, but after another grunt jumped in, we pushed his body and brains to one side so we'd have room enough to stay low. There wasn't anymore shooting that night, but I didn't sleep.

"Was I scared?" asked Slade. "You're damn right I was, but I'll tell you this, I've never really been afraid of anything since then."

In an attempt to salute Slade, Randy raised his beer mug and was surprised to find Slade clicking glass with him.

"Happy birthday, see you tomorrow," said Slade as Red Morrison approached to drive Slade, the eldest member of the Champs, back to Ashville.

"No more stops for us," said Morrison in the direction of Edward Champion, Irish and Schmidt, who had occupied themselves at the bar in a game involving shaking five dice from a circular, leather container.

A few minutes after Morrison and Slade had departed, Edward Champion shouted, "Last call for Red Bud" loud enough so the Champs, including any who might have been relieving themselves in a restroom, would not be left behind.

Chapter 17

Slade's knowledge of Randy's parents did not concern Randy because whether in Crown Point or in Ashville, he knew there were few secrets. As a result, while Johnny drove to Rosie's in Red Bud, Randy stretched out on the passenger side of the front seat and pulled his baseball cap's bill to just above eye level during Irish's return to story telling.

Even as a short time visitor to Ashville, Randy had accrued information from various visits to the front desk of Champion's. That's where Johnny filled in whatever blanks Randy had about not only Edward Champion, but Irish and Schmidt - all who had given no indication of being married.

With those three in his thoughts, Randy rested during the drive and recalled Johnny saying a few days earlier: "My mom was killed in a car wreck - a head on collision when I was five years old."

"She was going shopping at Christmas time and driving alone. She and my dad were born in 1904, the year of the World's Fair in St. Louis. They were high school sweethearts and got married right after graduation when my grandpa started grooming Dad to take over the store. Mom was only 39 when she died. Dad really took her death hard and never remarried.

"From what I heard about Irish, he had been married, but she left him for another guy. Somebody said the guy was an umpire in the St. Clair League. At one point, Irish bought a pistol from my dad's store and was going to kill the guy.

"A lot of people in town knew Irish's wife because she was a teacher at the high school. Everybody knew she was a knock out.

"As soon as Dad heard Irish had bought the gun, he found him, gave him his money back, and told him to go home and see if his wife was still there. Dad already knew she had left town with the umpire."

Regarding military service, Johnny indicated that both his dad and Irish were too young to get into World War I and too old for WW II, but Schmidt's story was different.

Accustomed to using the expression "somebody said," Johnny told how somebody said Schmidt had a wife, but she took off after a few years of working in the Foul Ball and having to live on the second floor of the building.

"His sister runs the place whenever he's not there," said Johnny.

Had Randy any question about Schmidt and the military, one of Irish's back-seat stories provided an answer prompted by a question linked to baseball.

"Didn't Schmidt hurt his back during a road trip like this?" Irish asked Edward Champion.

Without waiting for an answer, Irish continued, "It was after a non-league game in the '30s in Evansville, and after we made a stop just outside of town, some guy at the bar asked Dutch if he was the one who struck out five straight times in the game.

"We all knew Dutch was built like a bull, but he never did hit, so he tried to shut up the smart ass by making a bet that he could lift up the front end of an old Chevy parked outside the tavern.

"We all put in a buck to cover the bet and went outside where, sure enough, Dutch grunted and groaned and got the front wheels a few inches off the ground. He won the bet, but he also screwed up a disc in his back and was classified Four F by the military."

If Edward Champion had become bored by any of Irish's stories, the only indication was his saying, "Thank God" as Johnny pulled the Lincoln into Rosie's, which was larger than the previous establishments that had welcomed the Champs.

As Randy entered, he recognized additional contrasts. Rosie's was roomier due to the absence of a pool table and because it featured a hardwood dance floor in front of a glistening jukebox. Even more sparkling was the smile of the proprietor, a red haired, middle aged woman who immediately recognized Edward Champion, Irish and Schmidt, and embraced each before pouring drinks for the Champs.

An avid baseball fan, Rosie reminisced with the trio about years past, games and visits, but was caught by surprise when Edward Champion ordered Johnny to play something from the jukebox.

"You didn't forget, did you, Rosie?" asked Champion, who delighted in Johnny's selection and leaned toward Irish and Schmidt with whispered instructions.

Within seconds of "Hey Good Lookin" by Hank Williams, Rosie found herself in the arms of Irish, who twirled her about and lip synched the lyrics as they danced.

From a nearby table, and this time without instructions, Johnny mimicked strumming a guitar. Randy joined in by playing an imaginary bass fiddle, and other players followed by tapping their feet or trying to blend their singing with that of Williams as Schmidt cut in on Irish.

After the song reached concluding lines of "How's about cookin' something up with me?" Rosie turned to Champion, still seated at the bar, and asked if she could feed the boys.

"Nah, we're heading back to Ashville, and if anybody is hungry, Dutch will make them burgers at his place," said Champion.

Any indication of departure was welcomed by Randy, who by then had failed to balance his beer intake with popcorn, peanuts, and potato chips.

"Just get me home," was his slurred request to Johnny, who eventually led Randy up the back stairs of the sporting goods store and into his room.

"Don't forget, game tomorrow," said Johnny after Randy had removed his Levi's, T-shirt, shoes, and socks, and fell face down into the bed.

Chapter 18

Thanks to Johnny, the late June heat and humidity could not affect Randy as much as the tavern stops, beer, snacks and a swollen left elbow. By opening the only window in Randy's room and turning on the store's lone air conditioner, a one-room model resting in the window of Edward Champion's office loft, Johnny created air flow comfort for the birthday boy.

As a nearby church tower clock struck 1 a.m., Randy had no idea of the heat he was about to encounter.

Not willing to stumble in the dark of his room and across the hall to the bathroom to find aspirins, he remained in bed and was wavering in and out of sleep when he thought he heard a creaking noise from the back stairs.

Was he alert enough to think the stairs had settled after Johnny's departure?

Could a cat have found its way into the store and begun nocturnal investigations?

No need to consider that because from across the hall a light filtered from beneath the bathroom door and into his room.

Had he left the light on? Again, no need for consideration because as he rubbed his eyes and listened, he realized someone was taking a shower.

Turning slowly to an edge of his bed, he thought about grabbing a baseball bat for protection - a strategy which passed quickly after the shower had stopped and the bathroom door opened.

In the doorway, stood a woman whose youth and beauty may have been covered from knees to neck by a Baby Doll nightgown, but whose body was almost entirely revealed in a silhouette created by the bathroom light.

As she flicked moisture from her thick, dark hair, Randy tried to focus on her eyes, but found himself lowering his stare to her breasts, to her legs, and to her bare feet.

By the time he had asked, "Who are you? How'd you get in here?" she was only a few feet from him.

"Call me Ava," she responded while examining the room in its limited darkness.

"I'm Mr. Champion's niece, and I just got in from Macon, Georgia," she said with a southern accent that, as intended, seemed to put a northern boy at ease.

"I got a late start, and then had car trouble, so I thought I may as well come here instead of waking up Uncle Edward and Johnny at home."

"This is where I stayed last year," she continued. "I kept my key."

Realizing he was wearing only underpants, Randy failed in an attempt to cover himself with the sheet which had become twisted in his slumber. When he groped from a corner of the bed for the Levi's he had draped on the back of a chair, he found himself too late to prevent his visitor from reaching the pants and tossing them into a corner.

In the next instant, she placed one hand on his chest, and the other on his rippled stomach, and guided him back into bed where another surprise awaited him.

After sitting on the bed, she ran her fingertips across each side of his face, slowly touching his deep dimple and scar, and then began singing the lyrics from "Young at Heart," a popular song by Frank Sinatra.

"Fairy tales can come true, it can happen to you, if you're young at heart. For it's handy you will find, to be narrow of mind, if you're young at heart."

Whether relaxed due to what had become a long birthday celebration or unsure if he was dreaming, Randy gave no objection to having Edward Champion's niece near him.

Consequently, he failed to hear her quietly conclude, "And if you should survive to one hundred and five, look at all you'll derive out of being alive, and here is the best part, you have a head start, if you are among the very young at heart."

Chapter 19

Awakened by the drone of the air conditioner and then shook into reality by church bells chiming a dozen times, Randy knew he was alone. He also knew he did not want to be late for the Champs' game at the Athletic Field.

Putting on his uniform, he realized that even though he had hung it on a hanger behind his bedroom door, it carried the aroma of his late night visitor.

No time for breakfast he thought as he drove with lowered windows past one of the small restaurants where he had eaten on occasion, and no time for a clean No. 27 as he sped past a laundromat.

As a result of a 1 p.m. game time, he had a few minutes to compose himself, but as he entered the Athletic Field, he caught the fragrance of Ava's rosebud orchid perfume and saw her behind the home plate screen with Edward Champion.

"Randy, this is my niece, Georgia Ann Champion," was a surprising introduction that led to the brunette standing, smiling, lowering her sun glasses, looking into Randy's eyes, and saying in her southern most accent, "Delighted to meet you."

"She's visiting for a week," added Champion.

"My pleasure," said Randy during a handshake shortened by his looking toward the third base dugout where Red Morrison sought a bat to use for infield-outfield practice.

Moving quickly, Randy failed to hear Champion's niece add, "I've heard so much about you."

What Randy and his teammates did hear was a repeat of Morrison's concern about returning to a Sunday league game after playing at the prison. Mishandled ground balls and wild throws in the pre-game preceded a 7-1 loss to Shiloh featuring only a long home run by Slade.

Plagued by his ailing left elbow, Randy was hitless in four at-bats on two infield ground balls and fly balls to shallow right and center field. His throwing skills also suffered as evidenced in the ninth inning when he tried to cut down a runner at home plate only to overthrow the catcher and have the ball strike the screen in front of the Champions - uncle and niece who departed shortly thereafter.

Soundly beaten, the Champs' reprieve came in Morrison's reminder of the July 4th weekend, meaning non-league games against a Cape Girardeau, Missouri, team on Saturday and Sunday.

"And, don't forget Sunday is homecoming day at the Fairgrounds," said Morrison, whose reminder led to Randy asking Johnny for an explanation at the Foul Ball.

"Homecoming is a fund raising day for the city," said Johnny before taking a sip of soda which again became the drink of choice for Randy.

"Everybody is expected to contribute because the city gives the profits to the Recreation Department for Little League sports."

"Some of our players will work at various booths, but Dad wants you to report to the stage area by 7:30. That should give you time to get out of your uniform and shower. Just put on some khakis, a white polo shirt, and loafers like you do for work, and you'll be fine."

Tired from the events of consecutive days and irritated by his poor performance on Sunday, Randy left Johnny and the Foul Ball without asking anything else about the homecoming. Nor did he refer to the first name of Johnny's cousin or her snug pedal pushers and revealing blouse which had drawn numerous glances from the baseball players and spectators.

Chapter 20

Because the boss' niece, according to Johnny, was spending time sightseeing and shopping with her uncle in St. Louis, Randy returned to a week of work and deliveries without worry.

A dinner guest at times to Edward Champion's home just three blocks from the sporting goods store, Randy made sure Johnny understood that baseball had returned to the forefront and a free meal had become secondary.

After a successful Wednesday practice confirmed that Randy's elbow had healed, he was anxious to play against Cape Girardeau, a team Irish predicted could provide July 4th fireworks a day ahead of the homecoming extravaganza at the Fairgrounds.

Even though Bauer and Smith, normally outfielders, split the pitching duties on Saturday, the Champs appeared headed for victory. That was until the visitors' muscular catcher smacked a long, three-run home run over the center field fence in the seventh inning for a 6-4 victory.

Estimated by Irish at nearly 450 feet, the prodigious homer overshadowed Randy's three runs batted in on sharply hit singles.

"Longest home run hit here since Josh Gibson," Irish explained later to an audience at the Foul Ball.

"He was known as the black Babe Ruth and barnstorming in the early 40s with some other Negro league stars when they stopped in Ashville to play against St. Clair League players and other guys home from pro ball.

"The Negro league team was losing until about the eighth inning when our pitcher tried to sneak a fast ball past Gibson, and he hit it over 500 feet over the center field fence.

"Boy, did he live up to his nickname! The ball easily cleared the top of the 425-foot sign by a couple of feet, sailed over the hill behind it, and landed in the center of South Illinois Street.

"It bounced so high we could see it from the grandstands, and then it rolled right past a guy's car at the Zephyr filling station across the street."

If Irish's account of Gibson's mammoth blow seemed embellished, he had more fuel for expanded description on Sunday. Although Range hurled an outstanding game, he needed Randy's dramatic two-out, two-strike, two-run homer well above and beyond the right field fence for a 3-2 victory.

Due to the speed of the game, Randy felt fortunate as he recalled his promise to Johnny. After showering and putting on fresh clothes, he arrived at the Fairgrounds ahead of schedule, meaning he had to endure some of the events scheduled for the portable wooden stage which had been set up on the back of a flatbed truck.

Since the truck's cab was still attached, one of its exhaust pipes served as a pole for a clothes line stretched above and across the bed and fastened to a pole at the opposite end. Hanging from the line, several sheets formed a curtain and also provided a background blocking a view of a nearby concession stand.

Facing the stage, rows of wooden chairs held an audience of about 200 who warmly greeted the National Anthem played by the Ashville High School band, which performed from a grassy area near the truck's cab.

After hearing solo song performances by everyone from the mayor's daughter, to the Ashville High principal's son, to the off-key harmonica efforts of the school board president himself, Randy sat erect in his rear row seat as Edward Champion took the microphone.

"As many of you know, the Champs won today. Now I'd like to introduce to you the Anderson brothers who will try to explain the game of baseball for us all," said Champion. The middle infielders, dressed in baseball uniforms, then gave their rendition of Abbott and Costello's "Who's on First?".

Moments before Mark Anderson identified "I Don't Give a Darn" as the shortstop's name to further confuse his brother Sandy, Randy felt a tap on his shoulder. After following Johnny to the back of the stage, Randy was given a metal folding chair and told to be ready to take it on stage and sit close to the front edge.

As Edward Champion informed the crowd "of another baseball surprise on this marvelous holiday weekend," Randy did as he was told to the cheers of those aware of his game-winning homer.

Unaware of Champion's signal to the band, Randy also did not see behind him six women dressed in white tennis shoes, white baseball pants, red vests, and red, white and blue top hats.

He had become the center of attention. And, as the women sang, "You're our Yankee Doodle Randy, you're our Yankee Doodle boy," they danced around him in a routine reminiscent of movie star James Cagney.

By the time they reached "A real live nephew of our Uncle Ed," Randy was fully aware of Georgia Ann Champion, who outfitted him with a vest and top hat and then pulled him into the middle of the line of women for a leg-kicking routine.

With teammates hooting from beyond the stage, Randy blushed but persevered, knowing the women and the band were about to reach their final notes.

After bowing, and moving off stage with the group, he asked Georgia Ann, "Where'd you come from?"

Meanwhile, her uncle returned to the mike and spoke of "another treat".

As Georgia Ann and Randy walked down the steps from the flatbed, she tightly grabbed his hand, and said: "Y'all got to see this."

Apparently, she had contributed to planning the entertainment and done more than sightseeing and shopping during her visit.

Chapter 21

Still unsure if Edward Champion or Johnny knew of Georgia Ann as a birthday boy visitor, Randy remained resolute to the fact that she was the boss' niece, and he was not about to jeopardize his work or baseball.

Sitting next to her, he moved closer and asked: "Why'd you say your name was Ava?" only to hear her say, "I'll tell you later" as Johnny took the stage wearing his Champs' baseball uniform and carrying a banjo in his right hand.

Seated in the chair Randy had vacated and behind a lowered microphone, Johnny was joined by four wives of Champs' players. This time three wore the same uniforms as in the previous skit while the fourth wore black slacks and a black shirt and carried a chest protector ala an umpire.

With the women behind him, Johnny steadied the neck of his banjo with his left hand and strummed with his right while singing:

"One home run,
How I'd like to hit just one home run,
Circle the bases, have some fun
With one home run.

"One four-bagger,
How I'd like to show my swagger,
Dance and run, under the sun
With one home run.

During each stanza, the women mimicked a pitcher throwing to a batter positioned in front of a catcher and an umpire. Each time Johnny reached his last line, the batter would swing and hold her hand like a visor to her forehead as if to see how far she had hit the invisible pitch.

"Going deep,
How I'd like to bring the crowd to its feet,
Hold my head up high, point to the sky,
With one home run.

"Even in my sleep,
I see my jump and leap
After swinging a bat, and tipping my hat
With just one home run."

By the time Johnny returned to his first stanza, various members of the band had found the tune easy enough to provide accompaniment while the audience stood and swayed from side to side.

"Isn't he something?" Georgia Ann asked Randy, who had seen a piano in the Champion living room but had no idea of Johnny's musical talent.

Following the standing ovation for Johnny, a barber shop quartet took stage as Georgia Ann and Randy walked hand-in-hand toward an array of booths, including a baseball throw stand. Inside was Schmidt, wearing a black and white striped prison outfit and sitting in a wire cage above a barrel of water. When a thrown ball hit the target connected to Schmidt's perch, the tavern owner threw his hands skyward before being dunked.

As darkness approached, Georgia Ann pointed to a Ferris wheel and told Randy how it would provide an excellent vantage point from which to watch the fireworks display.

"Besides," she drawled, "there are some things I've got to tell you."

Chapter 22

When the youthful pair reached the .25 cents per ride Ferris wheel, Georgia Ann beat Randy to the punch with money, handed two dollar bills to the attendant, batted her eyes, and told him to let them ride until she signaled otherwise.

As their carriage ascended, Randy again referred to "Ava," bringing a reply from the brown-eyed beauty whose final accent laced words were, "My goodness, Randy, we must be telepathically linked. That was the first thing I wanted to talk about."

While the wheel turned through the summer heat of ground level and then into the cooler night air, Randy learned how a southern girl with no apparent needs became obsessed with Ava Gardner, the Hollywood movie star.

Like Randy and Johnny, Georgia Ann also was an only child. But as the daughter of Mr. Earl Champion, a prominent Macon, Georgia, attorney, she had everything a girl could want from childhood to college.

Meanwhile, Randy wondered, "Was it everything her parents could want for her?"

"They named me after a state," she said. "Why not just call me Peach Champion?" she asked before adding how she had been called her parent's 'little peach'.

Sent to the best of private schools, Georgia Ann ("Ann" representing her mother's first name) said she was "groomed for Southern aristocracy".

From the occasional parties when "Daddy" as she called him, would entertain local legal and political types, she learned as early as her grade school days how to properly conduct herself.

The only exceptions came when she would join her neighbor, Betty Sue Dixon, the daughter of a local physician, for short walks to Macon's Cox Capitol Theater. That's where the movie stars she had found in Betty Sue's magazines came to life.

"I can tell you everything about Ava Gardner," said Georgia Ann. "After Betty Sue and I saw her in the movies, Betty said I looked just like Ava, and I was hooked."

"Ava grew up in North Carolina. She was 19 years old - just like me now, when she visited her sister in New York and posed for a photo by her sister's husband who was a professional photographer.

"When a Hollywood talent scout saw the picture in the window of her brother-in-law's studio, everything changed for Ava - even her North Carolina accent.

"She's made movie after movie, and she's married to Frank Sinatra, but she can act better than Marilyn Monroe or Elizabeth Taylor. But I don't like the way those magazine gossip columnists call her a 'femme fatale'."

Unable to pronounce or define the French expression describing an alluring, seductive woman, Randy continued to listen, knowing the Ferris wheel had not yet made a full revolution.

"Well, since you asked about my name, I had to tell you, but I also wanted you to know I'm going back home tomorrow morning," said Georgia Ann, who then urged Randy to call her "Georgia".

"I've enjoyed being with you, Randy, but I want you to know today has been extra special," she continued.

"And it's not just because you joined the fun or because of my visiting you on your birthday night.

"It's because I knew Johnny was the one who approached his dad with the idea of playing the banjo, and it's Johnny, who after being told 'No,' showed his dad he doesn't have to lead his son's life.

"Maybe Johnny will run the sporting goods store someday, but after today, he's not going to be the boy who was held back in school because of his accident and because of the bullying he endured in grade school.

"I'm going back to Georgia and the university there where Daddy got his degree, but I'm not going to be the same sorority girl leading her life just to please everyone else.

"And, no more cooing for Georgia football recruits when I know all they can do around a woman is drool like the school's mascot, a big fat bulldog."

Whether spurred on by the shared smiles of the moment, or his appreciating her frankness and loss of accent, or by the view of the fireworks from the wheel's apex, Randy looked into Georgia's eyes, and kissed her.

"Georgia, meeting you has meant a lot to me," he said.

Responding without accented words but with accented feeling, she ran her right hand across his back, let him pull her closer, and returned his kiss.

"I know all about you, Randy Wilson," she continued. "Johnny told me everything, and I knew right away you were special.

"I also know you've got to keep playing baseball and go back to school."

After they kissed again, Georgia signaled for an end to the Ferris wheel ride, and gladly accepted Randy's offer for a ride in his Ford.

As they headed for the parking lot, the barber shoppers, harmonizing at a beer stand, entered the second stanza of their rendition of "You Are My Sunshine" with:

"The other night dear

As I lay sleeping

I dreamed I held you in my arms."

Chapter 23

Although higher temperatures dominated Ashville in July, the Champs remained in contention for first place in the St. Clair standings. As Randy tried to adjust to the weather, he also realized how much moisture his wool flannel uniform could retain.

It was one thing to deliver sporting goods in 90-degree weather but another trying to deliver base hits while sweating and swinging a 34-inch, 32-ounce wooden bat.

Fortunately for Randy, Red Morrison suggested the young slugger use a rosin bag to keep his hands dry, but the manager's story of a previous Ashville player was as valuable.

"Joe Schmidt hit .441 in 1939 for the Cardinals' Class D team in Duluth, Minnesota, and I never forgot what he told me about hitting," said Morrison before confirming that Schmidt was not related to Dutch Schmidt.

"I knew Joe was a great hitter in high school, but I had to know if there was any secret to his success as a pro.

"He said one of the things he and his teammates did any time they got a new Louisville Slugger was to break the neck of a soda bottle and then use a piece of the broken glass to shave the bat handle so it wasn't so slick.

"He also said some of the players who used bigger bats with thicker handles would cut grooves into the wood for a better grip.

"I know some of the fellas who play fast-pitch softball at South Side Park down the street from the Athletic Field have tried the same thing.

"What I get out of it is that things like this can help if you're already a good hitter."

Slade also provided advice for whenever the Champs played on fields lacking an outfield fence.

"A double to left center field is as good as one to right center," said Slade, who reminded Randy he did not have to pull every pitch to right field.

After hitting pitches on the outside corner of the strike zone to the opposite field during batting practice, Randy notched more than doubles in games at Mascoutah and New Athens.

Due to sun baked outfield surfaces, two of his liners that ordinarily would have been doubles at Mascoutah became home runs after each shot rolled between outfielders and to the edge of a corn field as Randy circled the bases.

At New Athens, similar occurred, but he added two home runs by lofting long fly balls to left field and into corn stalks whose location contributed to ground-rule homers, giving him four, four-baggers in four at-bats.

In addition, he made the defensive play of the game. With one out, the bases loaded, and the Champs leading 5 -3 in the eighth inning, he charged a low line drive, caught the ball just above the ground and continued running to second base where he tagged the bag to complete an unassisted double play.

"Dandy Randy Goes 4-for-4 Plus 1" was the Ashville News headline the next day after a performance impressive enough for Irish to notify the Associated Press office in St. Louis, which sent a brief, two paragraph account of the unusual accomplishments across the country.

The four homers and unassisted double play were tidbits earning Irish $10. Years earlier, he had impressed the AP by submitting an account of an Ashville Little League game in which he claimed a 10-year old batter may have hit one of the longest home runs in baseball history.

According to Irish, after the youngster hit a single to right field, a dog from a yard neighboring the baseball field ran onto the diamond and grabbed the ball with his teeth. When he was about 600 feet from home plate, the outfielder retrieved the ball, but by then the excited batter had scored.

For Randy, there was no home run in the July 26 all-star game at the Athletic Field where he was joined by Slade and Range. Plagued by a return to his habit of pulling pitches, he managed just two lazy outfield fly balls in his only at-bats.

Yet, if he contributed little to the St. Clair League's 7-5 victory over the Clinton County League, he had more to offer the Champs on the morning of the all-star game.

Even though he had been an Ashville resident for nearly two months, he was remiss in doing something he had known from childhood, going to Mass on Sunday. Bitterness over his parents' deaths or being on his own and away from St. John's Catholic environment should not have been excuses, things Randy considered as he entered the Ashville Cathedral just after the start of a 9 a.m. service.

Kneeling, he thanked God for being able to adjust to his new life and for his baseball talents creating optimism. His thoughts changed though when he heard the start of a sermon given by a priest who introduced himself as "Father William Grace Martin" and said he was "pleased to have found Ashville".

When the priest explained how the origin of his name was the result of having parents, William and Grace Martin, Randy momentarily dwelled on being named after his grandfather Randall Arthur Wilson.

Because of the brief sermon, Randy took advantage of the extra time before getting ready for the all-star game, remained kneeling, and returned to his personal prayers as other church goers departed. Left alone, he walked to the front of the Cathedral and was observing its statues and stained glass windows when he could not help but overhear dialogue from the vestibule.

"I'm the Monsignor here, not you. I don't care how much you love baseball. You're not here to serve up home run pitches. You're here to serve the church."

To which, in a voice recognized by Randy as that of Father William Grace Martin, came the reply, "Yes, Monsignor."

In the stillness of the church, Randy genuflected, made the sign of the cross, and walked toward the rear doors where he found a Sunday bulletin - something he thought would interest Johnny as well as Edward Champion.

Chapter 24

After delivering products into the early afternoon of Monday, July 27, Randy joined Johnny at Champion's in search of the Ashville News and found much for consideration other than the sports page.

"Armistice Signed; Korean War Ends" screamed a page one headline above details of the compromise of the war which had begun on June 25, 1950.

"Dad's going to be happy about that," said Johnny, recalling how the Champs had lost players to the Armed Forces, including some who had walked along the 38th parallel separating North Korea from South Korea.

Turning to the sports page to see Irish's account of the St. Clair all-star victory, Randy became captivated by a photo of the St. Louis Browns' third baseman tagging out a Boston Red Sox runner.

"Who's he look like, Johnny?" asked Randy, referring to the third baseman.

"Looks like Jim Dyck, or at least that's what the caption says," said Johnny.

"Baloney, he's the spitting image of Slade," said Randy before adding, "they almost look like twins."

After glancing again at the photo related to the Browns' double header split with the Red Sox in which Dyck helped the lowly St. Louis team end a seven-game losing streak, Randy continued.

"Come on, Johnny, there's meaning in that picture.

"Doesn't everybody know how Slade was one of the best hitters ever at Ashville High School, but never got a chance to play pro ball because he was drafted into the Army?

"I've heard your dad, Irish and Schmidt tell story after story of how he could hit a baseball, and how a Cardinals' scout watched him play in high school and with the Champs only to have Pearl Harbor hit before he could go to a tryout.

"Wouldn't it be something if Slade got his chance to play in the majors?"

"You been drinking beer again?" asked Johnny. "He's not about to play for the Cardinals!"

"I'm not talking about the Cardinals," said Randy, whose enthusiasm was sparked by thoughts related to a previous week night when he, Johnny, and Edward Champion watched the Cardinals at Sportsman's Park in St. Louis.

"We got to see Stan Musial hit against Warren Spahn, but don't you realize the Browns play in the same ball park?" asked Randy.

"You know where we sat near the dugout on the third base side? After the game, remember how the Cardinals walked to their clubhouse through part of the grandstand and then went out of view under the second level?

"The Browns do the same thing, but nobody bothers them. If we could intercept Dyck when he comes out of the clubhouse before a game, we could get Slade to take his place."

Caught by the idea, Johnny added to it, saying, "Get Slade into Dyck's uniform, and nobody'd know the difference. They're both about 6-foot-2 and 200 pounds."

"We need help, and here it is," said Randy pointing to Irish's byline.

"Didn't he say sometimes he's been an official scorer for the Browns?" asked Randy.

"He's got to know Mr. Veeck."

Even in Indiana, Randy had read of Bill Veeck, the eccentric Browns' owner, batting a midget in a 1951 game. Later, he hosted a "Grandstand Manager's Day" when the fans held up placards indicating "Yes" or "No" to the public relations director's proposed moves to steal or bunt or change pitchers.

"Why couldn't Irish get Mr. Veeck to go along with our idea?" asked Randy, prompting a series of concerns from Johnny.

"The switch would have to be made just before game time, and don't forget he'd have to play third base in the top of the first inning," said Johnny. "And, how do you get Dyck back on the field?"

"That's why I'm going to see Irish tomorrow," said Randy, who fell asleep that night envisioning Slade making a diving stop and then hitting a home run.

Chapter 25

When the call for Irish to report to the front office came over the recently installed intercom system at the Ashville News, he had been mulling over the St. Clair League rosters. President Mathews had dropped them off that morning, a day after the deadline for managers to make additions or deletions, but before meeting with Randy, Irish underlined the names of two new Champs' players.

One was Kent Keller, the player who had been cut prior to the season. The other was Billy Grace, whose name meant nothing to Irish.

Although the newspaper's lobby faced South Illinois Street, just a few blocks from the Athletic Field, the front of the building also offered a full view of the presses. At times, as on Monday when news of the Korean War Armistice spread, it was not unusual for a small crowd to gather in anticipation in ways similar to how people had gathered a few years earlier at an Ashville furniture store displaying an early model of the first television set.

On Tuesday, the lobby was quiet. In an adjoining room, Irish learned Randy's scheme to allow Slade an opportunity to have the professional baseball experience he never had.

"Sure, I've met Bill Veeck, and I'm well aware of his antics," said Irish after looking at the photo of Dyck which Randy had circled.

"You know he even had a ladies' day once when he gave them orchids flown in from Hawaii for attending a Browns' game. He's also had fireworks shot off after some games."

If citing Veeck promotions increased Randy's optimism, the feeling was short lived not because Irish doubted the Browns' owner would consider the player switch but for another reason.

"You're forgetting No. 1 in this," said Irish. "It's Slade."

"He's the concern here, not Veeck, or Dyck."

As Randy sat without response, Irish continued, "You may have played a few weeks of baseball with Slade and even spoken with him at times, but I don't think you really know him.

"He's got a wife and three kids, and this County League ball means more to him than anything else. What happened when he was younger is in the past.

"Who knows? Maybe he didn't get signed because someone in town told a scout he had a bad throwing arm or couldn't hit a curve ball.

"All I know is that Frank Slade doesn't give a damn about any of that any more than he cares if the Cardinals contend in the National League or if the Browns lose 100 games in the American League.

"What he cares about is having a chance to win a championship with the Champs, and to him and a lot of others, that's as big as the World Series."

As Randy weighed Irish's comments, he heard the roar of the nearby presses and leaned forward with a final request.

"Will you at least ask him?" insisted Randy.

"I'll do it tomorrow night," said Irish before asking, "Who's Billy Grace?"

Chapter 26

Intent on meeting Slade on Wednesday night at the Foul Ball, Irish failed to find Billy Grace, who was introduced to the Champs by Red Morrison at the team's weekly practice. Grace, who appeared to be in his early 30s, said he had moved into the area from Chicago and thought he could help the team because he was a left-handed pitcher. Aware of the previous introduction by Grace, Randy declined revealing the pitcher's identity.

According to Morrison, Grace and Kent Keller already had been given uniforms, had been added to the roster by Edward Champion, and were eligible to play immediately. At that point, whether Keller had been added due to a change of heart by Edward Champion meant little to Randy. More important was the presence of Grace, especially with four regular season games remaining prior to the St. Clair playoffs.

Apparently, Morrison also was concerned. After stressing the importance of "two good rounds of batting practice," the manager took Grace to the right field bullpen at the Athletic Field where he directed Keller to protect Koester, the catcher, from being hit by line drives while the new pitcher warmed up.

As Range tossed batting practice pitches to batters stationed at a plate placed in front of the screen behind home plate, Randy either hit, shagged fly balls or jogged across the outfield.

Whenever possible, he looked to the bullpen where Grace warmed up slowly. The lefty's fluid windup and fast ball did not appear to be anything out of the ordinary, but his curve ball was another story.

Its crispness and off-the-table trajectory had Koester often nodding approval after catching the pitch.

As the practice concluded, Randy spotted Slade speaking with Morrison and then departing, leaving an impression that the player had an excuse for not hanging around for the manager's comments.

Had Slade remained, he would have heard how the Champs were entering August in need of victories and in need of concentration.

"We have to play the next two Sundays on the road, and you can't be distracted," said Morrison.

"You know at St. Libory, they'll have cars parked off the diamond but on the first base side behind our bench where their fans will honk their horns every time the Saints get a hit or score a run. And, at O'Fallon, those planes flying overhead from Scott Air Base can affect us."

If those reminders brought smiles from the Champs, normally quiet first baseman Ted Hill forced more grins with his recall.

"Playing for a half barrel of beer at Millstadt didn't affect anybody, did it?" he asked.

"Remember when we played at Valmeyer in Monroe County last summer, and they had their players' wives and girl friends sun bathing just beyond the fence on the first base side?

"Now that was a distraction!" he said, adding to Morrison's effort to relax the team.

But if Randy and Johnny thought more relaxation awaited them at the Foul Ball, they were wrong. Upon entering the tavern, they found Irish sitting alone at a table and gesturing for them to sit down.

Chapter 27

If Randy and Johnny were anxious for Irish to have answers to their proposal, Slade's absence should have served as a foreshadowing.

"I got him to come over here because I told him we needed to talk," said Irish. "I hope he wasn't thinking it was for a column or feature story."

"I told him everything. Your plan, and that I've met Bill Veeck, and that the Browns are so bad, and Dyck is so underpaid, nobody would care. But I only got as far as making the switch, and Slade got up and walked out."

Supporting the brevity of the Irish-Slade meeting was a half-finished draft beer and full shot glass which remained on the center of the table.

"Do you think he's mad at us?" asked Randy. "All we wanted to do is give him a chance at something he never had."

Before answering, Irish slowly ran a finger around the rim of the shot glass, and said, "I just don't know. He could be pissed off. He could be mad at me for not writing more about him, or maybe he realized he was going to be late for work.

"Who knows? He could be pleased with your concern for him. He's always been quiet, but there always are questions. You just don't know what's around the next corner with him."

Not wanting to hear stories tied to memories at the Foul Ball, Randy and Johnny thanked the sports editor, but heard another question as they stepped from the table.

"Was Billy Grace there tonight?" asked Irish, who followed a dual response of 'Yes' by putting his head in his hands and saying, "Damn!"

If Irish had other questions related to the Champs, they were answered during August as the team confirmed his early optimism by sweeping two away games and then the final two home games to finish one game ahead of Freeburg for the regular season title.

Kept from witnessing the debut of Billy Grace and subsequent relief appearances due to covering the Ashville American Legion youth team in tournament games in East St. Louis, Irish got his chance on August 23 when the left hander relieved Range for three scoreless innings.

By then though, Irish had uncovered enough, including the pitcher's address on a contract provided by Mathews, to allow for a stunning sports headline in the August 24 Ashville News.

"Champs May Say 'Grace' in Playoffs" over a story disclosing Father William Grace Martin as "a pitching priest". Not only did the story draw the Monday morning attention of Randy and Johnny, it also made readers aware of the possibility of a championship game at the Athletic Field.

"Who's Shaughnessy?" Johnny asked Randy as they spread the sports section on the front counter.

"It says here St. Clair President Mathews has ruled that the league will follow the Shaughnessy playoff system in the first round starting Sunday, and then play a championship game on September 6."

"Must be the guy who came up with 1 vs. 4 and 2 vs. 3," answered Randy before offering his own question.

"Who's Ronnie Warren?"

The answer came in an Irish feature story indicating Freeburg would be aided by the return of former Freeburg High School star Warren, who was recently released by the Chicago Cubs.

"I think he's one of those 30-day minor-league wonders Dad talks about," said Johnny referring to players signed to a pro baseball contract but released on the 29th day so a team did not have to pay them more money or extend their contract.

According to Irish, "The 19-year-old Warren, who averaged 12 strikeouts a game in high school, had the fast ball of a major leaguer but was too wild for the Cubs."

"Dad said he had a million dollar arm, and a ten-cent brain," Johnny added.

Enthused by the chance of facing Warren, Randy knew he would not get an opportunity unless the Champs defeated fourth-place Lebanon in the first round, and Freeburg eliminated third-place New Athens, who had upset the defending champions in the regular season.

"If we get that far, the championship game will be in Ashville," said Johnny, unaware of a question which had plagued Randy in August.

"Where's Becker?" Randy asked himself before returning to another work day he had hoped would move quickly while baseball and the Champs occupied his thoughts.

Chapter 28

As the black Buick pulled into a parking space off a road within view of the baseball diamond at Lebanon, Charlie Becker wanted to be sure his car was out of foul ball range but close enough to observe the game.

His prized possession, the Roadmaster was a gift related to his contribution to Cleveland's 1948 World Series championship. After all, it was his recommendation to R. W. Johnston that led to the Indians acquiring pitcher Gene Bearden from the Yankees in 1946.

A World War II Navy shipmate of Bearden, Charlie knew left hander Bearden had pitched professionally before the war but also knew of his courage. Injured during a torpedo attack in the Solomon Islands in 1943, Bearden suffered a crushed right knee cap, twisted ligaments in his leg and a skull fracture but returned to the minor leagues in '45. He not only won 15 games that season in Class A but 15 more the next season in the Pacific Coast League.

Despite being on a Cleveland staff including future Hall of Famers Bob Feller, Bob Lemon and Satchel Paige, Bearden had a 20-7 record and a league-leading 2.43 earned run average.

After spotting Randy in center field, Charlie wondered if the college player could become a scout's dream and lead to another reward making up for the hours of travel and low pay.

Watching Randy belt hit after hit and then roam with ease for fly balls stirred Charlie's interest, especially since the outfielder's play supported a telephone call from Edward Champion, who spoke about his player's league-leading .400 batting average and 12 home runs in 15 games.

"First in batting average and with power. He'd be valuable in any league," thought Charlie although the player he had seen at St. John's was maturing even during the 8-2 playoff victory.

Unlike his collegiate games, this one involved a Lebanon bench warmer who called Randy everything from "pretty boy" to "scar face" to "dandy fanny" only to have each at-bat lead to or account for another Champs' run.

Obviously, the bench jockey had read the Ashville News, but on the last day of August, Monday, August 31, Irish had fodder for stories prior to the playoff finals after Freeburg routed New Athens, 9-1, in a game in which Warren struck out each of the nine batters he faced.

According to the game information Irish received from the Freeburg scorekeeper, "Warren was sensational, throwing flaming fast balls and sharp curves."

More important was the former Class D pitcher being comfortable as a relief pitcher – something he had not done during his brief stay in the Cubs' organization.

By coincidence, the Champs found comfort in Billy Grace hurling three innings at Lebanon in place of Range, who welcomed the rest after starting nearly every regular season game.

"Could be the best St. Clair championship game ever," Irish said in his "Brew" column which also indicated the game one day prior to Labor Day would include many "labors of love and baseball."

Among the plans of league president Mathews, Edward Champion and the Freeburg officials were food and drink concessions, a color guard from Scott Air Force Base to present the United States flag prior to the game, and an introduction of players over a public address system that would be used for the first time since the Stags played at the Athletic Field.

Practice for the Champs on Wednesday included team members doing everything from dragging the infield, to cleaning the dugouts, to sweeping the grandstand seats clean before being reminded by Morrison, "Sunday was for the Champs."

Chapter 29

In contrast to his first visit to the Athletic Field three months earlier, Randy experienced surprise on championship Sunday when he guided his car into the parking lot where he noticed two women on their knees with children nearby in the grass at the edge of the creek.

Wanting to discount the possibility of a problem, he approached one of the women who he recognized as Range's wife.

"Whenever he pitches, I always have to find a four leaf clover," she said, putting Randy's mind at ease.

As he entered the ball park, he approached Edward Champion and Charlie Becker, who occupied two of three folding chairs in the area normally reserved for the team sponsor.

"I saw you at Lebanon, but I didn't want to disturb you," said Charlie. "Hell of a game, and Mr. Champion says I can expect more today."

After shaking hands with both men, Randy expressed thanks for his summer opportunity and informed them he intended to leave for St. John's in the morning.

Before then though, the business of baseball was about to resume with batting practice for both teams. Meanwhile, Irish and Mathews tested two speakers on opposite sides of a scorer's table in the middle of the grandstand behind the home plate backstop.

Aware of Becker's presence, Randy performed no differently than before any other St. Clair game and laced line drives to all fields off batting practice pitches. But if his skills seemed impressive, they were matched later by Freeburg's slugging first baseman Boomer Walker, who supported his first name and regular season RBI title.

During pre-game infield and outfield drills, the smell of pop corn spread through the stands from a tent on the third base side where Dutch Schmidt also manned a makeshift grill. As fans filed in on what Irish, acting as an announcer, called, "a sun kissed Sunday," the sports editor reminded his audience there was no admission charge although hats would be passed around for contributions at the start of the seventh inning.

Apparently, a frustrated broadcaster, Irish mimicked Cardinals' announcer Harry Caray by saying, "Holy Cow!" before adding his own, "What a beautiful day for baseball!"

Shortly thereafter, he introduced Mathews, the umpires, and the teams whose members stood at attention with the spectators when the Air Force color guard posted colors and the Ashville Grade School choir sang the National Anthem.

After Mathews threw out a ceremonial first pitch, Range and Freeburg starter Eddie Lanter scattered hits in a scoreless duel until the sixth inning when they both became wild. Two base on balls preceded a long home run over the scoreboard by Freeburg's Walker. A walk and a hit batsman set up Slade's bomb to the front porch of a house across the street from left field.

Although the result was a 3-3 tie, Irish enjoyed the opportunities to use his home run call of "Oh my, goodbye" for Walker and then for Slade.

To support Irish's prediction, the game's outcome was turned over to relief pitchers Grace for the Champs and Warren for Freeburg - the former whose slow curve might have had God's blessing, and the latter who knew a major-league scout was sitting next to Edward Champion.

Word of mouth also accounted for the common knowledge that seated on the other side of Champion was Monsignor Patrick O'Donnell, who bent forward with each Grace pitch. Whether viewed by Randy from center field or from the on deck area, the Monsignor in his black garb seemed stoic.

In the top half of the ninth inning, perceptions yielded to the reality of a shocking collision.

With runners at second and third and two outs, Grace induced Walker into a soft fly ball into shallow left field where outfielder Bauer's hesitation to call for the ball and the speed of shortstop Anderson led to the players running into one another. After Anderson's right shoulder dug into the diving Bauer's right knee, the shortstop slid face down along the grass, but was able to hold onto the ball with his glove hand as Bauer came to rest in a heap two yards away.

Even before the base umpire reached the downed players, it was apparent their injuries would prevent them from playing the remainder of the game. That became obvious when Morrison signaled for Edward Champion to go to the Foul Ball and phone for an ambulance.

As the injured players were placed on stretchers, Mathews asked Irish if he thought the Champs were finished?

Without the aid of American Legion players who could have filled the Champs' late-season roster according to league rules, Edward Champion suddenly realized his selection of his son and Kent Keller had become paramount.

However, even if they failed as batters, how could they help defensively? Keller would move to shortstop, but Johnny would be in left field where he'd have to prove he could catch a fly ball, or, if necessary, make an accurate throw.

Chapter 30

After order was restored in the tied game, Irish announced that Keller would bat fifth and Champion sixth for the Champs. Prior to reaching those batters, Randy would lead off against Warren, who had breezed through the previous two innings just as he had in the playoff semifinal, and Slade would be in his usual cleanup spot.

Despite the doom related to the injured players, Randy found hope before his first at-bat against Warren as Slade walked into the on-deck area.

"When he kicks high, it's a fast ball," said Slade, who had mentioned little else to Randy after the proposal for the player switch at a Browns' game.

Sure enough, after Warren's high leg kick, Randy readied for a fast ball and whacked a long foul over the right field fence. On the next pitch, the kick was lower, and a curve ball became a called strike.

Another high kick preceded a line shot to right center field where the game took on another strange aspect when the ball struck a fence post and bounced directly to the Freeburg outfielder who was able to hold Randy to a long single.

"Would Slade guess fast ball and end this thing?" thought Randy.

The answer on the guess was yes, but the subsequent smash failed to clear the leaping Freeburg third baseman's outstretched glove and glanced away into shallow left field, allowing Slade to reach first base and leaving Randy as the winning run at second.

"Batting fifth for the Champs, No. 21, Kent Keller," announced Irish, causing the Freeburg second baseman to approach the pitcher's mound and speak with Warren.

"Just throw strikes. This kid can't hit, and look who's after him," said the infielder. "Get out of this, and there's no way they can stop us."

As instructed, Warren threw three consecutive fast balls past Keller, who failed to muster a swing.

"Next," said Warren loud enough for the Champs' fans and players to hear.

Whether insulted by having to pitch to the handicapped son of the sporting goods store owner and team sponsor or anxious because a scout was in attendance, Warren seemed in no need for more motivation.

Nonetheless, as Irish announced, "Batting sixth for the Champs, No. 30, Johnny Champion," the second baseman told Warren, "You know he has no business in this game; strike his ass out."

Close enough to overhear, Randy took advantage of the pitcher's intensity and secured a comfortable lead. Using his speed, he easily stole third base as Johnny stood with the bat on his right shoulder, and the umpire called, "Strike one!"

If Randy's strategy had been to draw a wild throw by the catcher, it failed. Now, with one out, he danced off third base, but his movement meant little as Warren threw an even faster pitch toward the inside part of the plate.

Fearful of being hit by the pitch, Johnny quickly leaned back, but in doing so accidentally swung his right hand and the baseball bat into contact with the ball that became a looping fly down the first base line and out of the first baseman's reach.

If the ball miraculously fell fair, it would become a game-winning single.

However, the second baseman knew his angle on the ball might allow him to catch it. But why attempt a catch? If the ball fell into foul territory, it would be just that - a foul ball, leaving Randy at third base and Slade at first.

If the ball were caught in fair or foul territory, the play could allow Randy to tag up and score the winning run.

That conjecture changed though when the third baseman shouted, "He's not tagging up!"

Hearing such caused the second baseman to run after the fly ball, catch it knee high - just above the foul line and begin a pivot for a throw to home plate.

What the infielders had not taken into account was Randy's reaction allowing him to return to third base, tag it, and sprint home.

Although the second baseman's throw appeared accurate, the ball took a hop toward the first base side of home plate. Alertly, Randy slid on the third base side and beneath the catcher's tag, igniting cheers from the Champs' fans and players.

As Red Morrison ran from the third base coach's box to home plate to congratulate Randy, players leaped from the Champs' dugout and raced to first base where a wide-eyed Johnny was lifted to Slade's shoulder and carried back to the plate for an extended celebration.

"Holy Cow!" screamed Irish while Mathews moved with trophy in hand down the grandstand steps and past Edward Champion, who was in the midst of a backslapping hug with Monsignor O'Donnell.

"Congrats to the new St. Clair League champions - the Champs," said Irish, who took advantage of the moment to close with, "If you don't believe it, you can read all about it in the News".

Chapter 31

Approached by Charlie Becker after the game, Randy appreciated hearing that the scout would return to St. John's in the spring.

"Great job," said Charlie. "You've improved as a player, and according to Mr. Champion, also matured off the field.

"Keep it up, and I'll recommend you to the Indians," he added as Randy departed for the Foul Ball.

Once inside, he enjoyed two bottles of Coca-Cola while learning Schmidt had won over $100 dollars in bets with some of the staunch Freeburg fans. He also overheard Mathews explain how Edward Champion had insisted on adding Kent Keller and the priest to the roster.

Regarding Father Grace, Randy asked if the league president thought the priest would be in trouble with Monsignor O'Donnell?

"I think Edward Champion took care of that with a donation," said Mathews while raising a hand and rubbing his index finger and thumb together.

After bidding farewell to his teammates, Randy returned to the sporting goods store where he showered, packed his clothes and used the silence of his room to help him compose a letter of thanks to Edward Champion and a letter of thanks and encouragement to Johnny.

In the morning, even though the store was closed, Randy met Johnny at the front desk where there would be no sharing of the Ashville News since the paper did not publish on the holiday.

"Just mail me a copy of the sports page," said Randy before handing Johnny the two letters as well as the key to the back door.

"We made a lot of memories," said Johnny, whose eye contact and strong handshake left impressions which Randy carried during his return to St. John's.

From Ashville to Collinsville and as he drove his Ford past Benld and north on Route 66, he had multiple thoughts:

"Would Johnny go to college and eventually take over his dad's business? Or would he do something like his cousin Georgia and find his own way? Would he become a musician or a successful song writer? Would he be Randy's link to Georgia?"

While observing how the farm fields had been harvested since his previous trip, Randy also wondered about Charlie's reference to maturity.

"Does maturity come from being a .400 hitter and winning games? Is it linked only to age? Does it come from experiencing a parent's death? Or, from occasionally swinging and missing but learning to adjust?"

After being on his own in Ashville, he recalled his experiences, and asked himself, "Could a single have as much impact as a home run?"

Then, he began to weigh his future.

"Getting a college degree was a priority, but did he really have a chance of playing pro baseball?"

After reaching Watseka, Illinois, not far from the Indiana border on Route 24, he stopped for gasoline, purchased an ice cream cone, and replaced musing with plans for the new school year.

Arriving at the main entrance to St. John's, he was eager to become reacquainted with the buildings destined to become his home for the next nine months.

After parking close to the recreation building, he could see his dormitory and the baseball field. Then his eyes captured a leggy blonde's descent from the roof where several coeds were sun bathing.

"Here's a letter for you, Dandy. Hope you had a nice summer," she said, handing him an envelope. He quickly opened it and learned he was invited to a Senior Class meeting on Tuesday night.

"Hey, did you call me 'Dandy'?" he asked to no avail as she turned away and began her return trip to the roof.

With increased curiosity, he looked closer at the letter and found it signed by Marilyn Johnston, Class of '54.

By the time he could say, "Thanks, Marilyn," she was near the top step but close enough to catch his smile and admiring stare. "See you tomorrow," she said.

Placing the envelope in his shirt pocket, he walked past the baseball diamond and toward his room. "One home run," he sang without knowing had he been able to compare his letter to the one the scout had received in May, he would have noticed how the "M" in Marilyn had an identical loop to each "M" in Mickey Mantle's name.

"How I'd like to hit just one home run," he continued...